Lock Down Publications and Ca$h
Presents

I'MMA DIE BOUT MINE

6

LET BLOOD RAIN

I0666778

By
Aryanna

First Edition 2025

Printed in the United States of America

Lock Down Publications
P.O. Box 944
Stockbridge, GA 30281
www.lockdownpublications.com

Like our page on Facebook: Lock Down Publications
www.facebook.com/lockdownpublications.ldp

Stay Connected with Us!

Text **LOCKDOWN** to 22828 to stay up-to-date with new releases, sneak peaks, contests and more…

Like our page on Facebook:
Lock Down Publications

Join Lock Down Publications/The New Era Reading Group

Visit our website:
www.lockdownpublications.com

Follow us on Instagram:
Lock Down Publications

Email Us: We want to hear from you!

Dedication

This book is dedicated to Lakia because you bring out the nerd in me, and I love you for it.

Acknowledgements

I thank God more and more every day for each gift he's given me, especially when it comes to my talents. I wanna thank my fans because as I get older, I really understand how much you mean to my growth, success, and my desire to keep doing what I do. It wouldn't be fun without you. I wanna thank BIG MAMA, my queen, who keeps me balanced and on top of the world when everything else is crashing down around me. I love you, sweetheart (pinky promise). I wanna thank my family for their love and support, especially my Big Byrd. You're a great mom, and I'm sooooo proud of you! Shout out to little Marcus, my favorite nephew! I wanna thank anyone who had anything to do with my success on any level. I appreciate it, for real. Shout out to my little man, Asaiah, aka, Peanut! I love you, son, and you'll know just how much one day. Shout out to my real ones behind the g-wall holding shit down day in and day out. Don't think that I don't feel your pain because I promise you that I do. I ain't never forgot a day of my bid, just like I ain't forgot the real ones I met along the way, and you all know who you are! As for you fake MF, who always wanna be messy bout some shit, I'mma need you to fall the fuck down and stay there. Save a nigga a bullet and a life sentence. Smh. Shout out to Lockdown Publications for this amazing run we've been on!! We got a decade together!!!

Chapter 1

(Fathergod)
(Texas)

I could feel my rage reaching its boiling point when it came to the Honorable Judge Jason Nathaniel because despite him knowing how serious I was, he refused to bend to my will. Not many mortals had made such a blatantly stupid decision, and the ones who did damn sure weren't around to talk about it.

"Judge, I detest repeating myself, but for the sake of your innocent children's lives, I'm gonna give you one more chance to right your wrong. You need to release the woman that you know as Tynesha Bishop because you know that her real name is Tesha Walker. If it's money that you're worried about then look no further because you will be well compensated. You have no one to fear more than me and my family so make the right decision," I advised.

It was normal for my 6'5", two hundred eighty pounds to intimidate a muthafucka when he could simply see me from a distance, so the way that I was looming over the judge after killing his wife and sister in front of him should've been terrifying. Sure enough, I could see the terror in his eyes, but my instincts told me that I wasn't the cause of it. Something or someone had this man more terrified than me, and I found that to be as intriguing as it was maddening because it put me at a disadvantage for the first time in thirty years. The pleading look in the judge's eyes was unnerving, which caused me to raise my gun and deposit four bullets into his face. His death was quick and painless, but it brought me no joy, and what was worse was the fact that it put me back at square one on how to solve one of the issues preventing me from making my family whole again. I left the judge's bullet riddled, badly beaten body strapped to the chair as I stepped over his wife's corpse on my way to the kitchen.

The ranch style house that the lovely couple had owned was spacious and isolated, sitting way out in the country on five acres. That meant that the bodies I was leaving inside could go undetected for weeks. I needed more immediate gratification though. When I got to the kitchen, I quickly snatched the stove away from the wall, disconnecting the gas and allowing it to begin its silent exploration throughout the house. I took my time walking back outside to the waiting black Ford Expedition, but instead of climbing inside, I went to the back and opened the trunk.

"How did it go?" Free asked from the backseat.

My grunt was enough to make her turn back around, and neither Destiny nor Angel said anything because I was sure they knew it was unnecessary. I pawed through the weapons cache we'd brought with us on our trip through Mexico until I came across the grenade launcher, and then I pulled it out. I stood on the side of the SUV and counted to sixty slowly, and then I pumped two grenades through the living room windows. The explosion was deafening, and the pressure from it pushed me up off my feet against the SUV. I was able to regain my balance before I hit the ground, but I could still feel the earth moving beneath my feet. The warmth from the flames caused my body temperature to rise, but it didn't thaw the frost around my heart. I quickly hopped in the backseat, and Angel pulled off fast.

"Do we go after his kids?" Free asked.

"Nah, it's no point in it now. We've gotta figure out another way to get Tesha out of that hospital," I replied.

"We could just break her out. I mean, I know that it's a secure facility, but it ain't like prison with guard towers and guns," Destiny said, turning around in the front seat and looking at me.

"I'm trying to avoid using that kind of force," I said.

"Since when?" Angel asked.

"Since Madeline asked me to," I replied with a sour taste in my mouth.

"I get it. She wants you to keep a low profile because dead men wage war, and the last thing we need is for you to go back to the top of America's most wanted list," Free surmised.

"Yeah, yeah, whatever. Tesha is family, and we do what we gotta do to bring her home. Royal needs her," I said, growing more frustrated by the second.

Despite the best doctors saying that he might never come out of the coma that was caused by the car accident in Switzerland six months ago, I was holding out hope that it just took the right person to bring my son back. I knew the love that Tesha and Royal shared, so I knew that if anyone could convince Royal to return to us then it would be her or their daughter, Stormy.

"Where are we going, Dad?" Angel asked as we came to a stop at a red light.

The contemplation of the answer wasn't due to a lack of options. It was me trying to decide what the best move was right now. The flare that had just gone up with regards to the judge and his family would cause immediate pressure, but there was no reason for the authorities to be looking in our direction. Of course, if we made a direct play toward getting to Tesha then the pieces of the puzzle might start to look clear to the cops. It was not just the cops though. It would be the Feds who descended on the state of Texas to hunt the ones who would dare kill a judge and his family. It was a risk, but what wouldn't we risk for family?

"We gotta get back out of the country before the Feds drop a net," I replied.

"So, we head back to Mexico," Free said.

"Not before we get Tesha," I said.

"So, what are you saying, Dad?" Destiny asked.

"I'm saying that Madeline is gonna be pissed, but she'll get over it. How far away is the mental hospital that Tesha is locked up in?" I asked.

"Uh... according to GPS, it's two and a half hours away because it's in Waco, Texas," Destiny replied.

"Let's go then," I instructed.

As we pulled off, I took my phone out of my pocket and tried to formulate my explanation to my wife before I made the call or sent the text. I had no doubt that she would understand because deep down, she knew what type of nigga I was when it came to family, but the fact that I'd promised her that I'd keep the violence to a minimum was what she'd focus on. It hadn't been my intention to make the streets run with blood, but I knew no limitations when my family was in danger, and I was unapologetic for that. Seeing the picture of Madeline and our daughter, Truth, as my wallpaper gave me even more of a reason to pause though. So many promises had been made to both of them about a life that didn't involve violence and running from the law, yet there I was, leading us down the familiar path.

"Sometimes forgiveness is all that you can ask for because permission isn't possible," Free said softly.

When I looked to my right at her, I saw clear understanding in her eyes, reflected by the moonlight. It helped with the foreign feelings of guilt that were weighing on me. My darkest fear was that my daughter, Truth, wouldn't understand me or be able to accept the things that I'd done once she was old enough to understand. I didn't wanna raise her like I had Freedom, Angel, and Destiny, where violence was accepted and expected. I wanted Truth to maintain her innocence and hold on to some of the illusions of the world being a good place. I decided to take Free's advice by not calling or texting Madeline, and instead, I put my attention elsewhere.

"Any word on Stormy?" I asked.

"The African government still refuses to acknowledge Royal as her father despite what the birth certificate says, especially now that David's DNA tests have been made a part of the official records in that country. Stormy's birthright makes her a princess and royalty just like her other siblings. I don't know of any country that's gonna turn over a royal to extended family when the parents are still alive," Free replied.

"So, we kill David and Tynesha, and we get Stormy back," Destiny reasoned.

"That won't get her back. That'll cause a fucking international incident," Free stated.

"Shit, it wouldn't be the first one we've caused," Angel replied.

"Nah, we not doing that," I said.

"Okay, so what's the plan?" Destiny asked.

"Honestly, Baby Dee, I don't have one because the only way that this is gonna work is with David's cooperation. I don't know the lil nigga to like him, but as a father who's always wanted to be a father. I can't just take that man's child from him," I replied.

"Even if you know that's what Tesha would've wanted?" Free asked.

"I know what Tesha wanted, but that don't mean that I necessarily agree with it. I miss my granddaughter as much as any of you, but David ain't the enemy that we need to fight head on right now, not about his daughter. Especially because we don't know where Marta is, and that fucking booby trap she had rigged to Royal's heart is still active. Every doctor that has examined Royal has said the same thing about the bomb connected to his heart being tamper proof, and the only way not to kill him while removing it is to find the muthafucka who put it there. For that information, we need Marta, so where are we at with finding her?" I asked, shifting thought processes.

"Well, we know that she was smart, and Interpol was dumb, because in order to beat the Red Notice that had been issued for her detainment, she just turned over Tynesha's son. After that, she vanished, and nobody has been able to track her down," Destiny replied.

"Are David's people searching for her?" I asked.

"I have no doubt, but there hasn't been any chatter about her being captured or killed, and something tells me that this is personal enough to Tynesha that it would be breaking news in every country," Free replied.

"Okay, so where do we think she is?" I asked, growing frustrated by the lack of reassuring answers.

"Colombia is our best bet because that's where she's from, and undoubtedly, that's where she'd feel the safest," Free said.

I didn't like this answer any more than I did the ones that came before it because I didn't have a foothold or any associates in Colombia. The resources that I would've tapped into when I'd still been a leader in the Black Gorilla Family had dried up with the organization's indictment season. I couldn't apply the right amount of pressure because technically, I was out of the game now. The only option that left me was to spend an obscene amount of money to buy the needed information, but the question was who could I pay for it?

"There's only one person that I can think of that will probably know where Marta is," Free said.

"Okay... well, don't keep me in suspense," I replied, looking at her.

"As badly as she wanted her father broken out of prison, I'd say that there's no way in hell that he don't know where she is," Free stated with a familiar certainty.

"Dad, you always knew where we were and what we were doing," Angel reminded me.

"And no matter where she's at, she's still the active leader of the Zeta Cartel," Destiny chimed in.

Everything that they said made logical sense, and it gave me an idea of which direction I needed to throw some money. I immediately sent Madeline a text informing her that I needed some serious strings pulled to get me inside of ADX Florence super max prison in Colorado for a private conversation with an inmate there. I already knew how huge this request was, but given the fact that Madeline was a former military general who'd been in charge of Guantanamo Bay, I was confident that she knew which back doors to sneak me through. With that play in motion, I turned my attention back to the current mission we were on.

"Baby Dee, give me a layout of the hospital that we're headed to," I instructed.

After a few moments of silence, the phone in my hand beeped, and I was looking down at the blueprints to Ridge Crest Mental Institution.

"It looks like they've had some recent renovations done, but whatever it was ain't showing up on the blueprints," Destiny said.

I saw the markings that had been made to plans indicating changes had been made, but there were no explanation or pictures provided for us to know what it meant. All I could do was study what I had and then adjust our attack according to whatever new shit was added to the maze. Based on the blueprints, there was an entire wing dedicated to housing the female patients, and it was on the opposite end of the building. Knowing where we were headed was the good part, but having to go through the men's ward was the bullshit that I didn't wanna deal with. I kept my mind occupied with different plans of attack for the entire ride, but once we pulled up, I knew that an easy job had just turned into mission impossible.

"So much for it not being a prison," Angel said.

Looking out of the front window, I knew that she was talking about the tall ass guard tower that had been erected outside of the fifteen feet high, chain link fence. Of course, the fence had signs posted warning of high voltage too.

"Who owns this place?" I asked, thinking of another way to attack this problem, while studying the structure for any obvious weaknesses.

"It's a state-run facility... Or at least it was up until a few months ago, and then it was bought by a private company," Destiny replied, tapping rapidly on her laptop.

"Tell me more," I said, feeling something pulling at my intuition about who the owner of this place actually was.

"I can feel you thinking, old man. What's up?" Free asked.

"It's no coincidence that somebody bought this place right around the time that Tesha was civilly committed here," I replied, giving her a knowing look that I knew she could read through the darkness.

"It does sound calculating when you put it like that," Angel said.

"Sounds like some shit we would do," Destiny commented.

"Nah, it sounds like what we *should've* done," Free corrected in a tone laced with self-disappointment.

"We can play the blame game later. For now, we just need to confirm our suspicions," I said.

"Okay, well, the company that owns the facility and the surrounding land is..."

The sudden spotlight that hit our SUV froze the words coming from Destiny's mouth as night suddenly became day. None of us got the chance to question what the fuck was going on though before the first bullet shattered the windshield.

"Drive, Angel!" I yelled, pulling my gun out and searching the surrounding darkness for a target.

Within seconds, it became clear that the shots were raining from above, like the devil was breathing fire with intent. Based on the booming sounds that followed the slugs rocking the SUV on its springs, I was guessing that it was .50 caliber slugs kicking and screaming at us. Given where the shots were coming from, it was impossible for us to return fire, so I just pulled Free close to me in hopes of shielding her while Angel pulled away fast.

"Dad! Oh, my God, Dad!" Angel screamed.

"It's okay, Angel, just drive," I instructed.

"No, Daddy. It's-it's Destiny!" Angel yelled hysterically.

I could still hear the shooting, but it was fading the farther away we got, so I took the risk of letting Free go to make sure Destiny was okay. I saw the blood on the seat first, and then I saw the look in my baby's eyes. The once dominant twinkle that had brought me so much joy was gone. My destiny was forever shattered and broken... because my baby was dead.

Chapter 2

(David)
(Ghana, Africa)
"Bae, what are you doing? Come back to bed."

When I took my eyes away from the window and looked back at what awaited me on the king-sized mattress, I felt more than temptation coursing through my veins. There was a certain tranquility too. Nobody was under the illusion that the storm was over, but we'd agreed to enjoy the parting of the clouds for a moment and just live life. Tomorrow wasn't promised.

"Come here for a minute... both of you," I said before turning my eyes back out to the patio below my bedroom window.

A few seconds later, Tynesha stood in all her naked glory on one side of me, and Carrie stood equally naked on my other side. Below us all of the children that we shared were playing with their aunts and cousins, and I could see out the corners of my eyes the smiles that appeared on both woman's face.

"Peaceful," Ty said.

"And so adorably innocent," Carrie added.

"That's all that we as parents could hope for, and it's our responsibility to make sure that things stay this way," I said.

"I agree... but in order for that to happen, you're gonna have to continue to keep us both happy too," Ty stated seriously.

"Is that right?" I asked.

"It definitely is," Carrie replied, taking my hand in hers and pulling me back toward the bed.

The thought flashed through my mind, questioning how this had turned into my life, but the reality that I was a king with a queen and a concubine was impossible to ignore. The crazy thing was that this hadn't been my idea. It was something that Tynesha and Carrie had come up with on their own in order to redefine what our family meant. Secretly, part of me believed that they'd come up with this agreement to spite Shaomi in the afterlife and Tesha, who was stuck in a mental institution. Either way, I wasn't complaining. When we got to the bed, Carrie pushed me on my back and climbed on top of me.

"I want his face," Ty said, climbing on the bed from the side.

"I'll gladly take the dick," Carrie said, using her soft hand to quickly stroke me to life.

Ty straddled my face and lowered her delicious pussy so that the breakfast fit for a king could be served. Carrie swiftly slid down my dick, impaling herself willingly as she reached out toward Ty. Together, they balanced each other out by holding hands as one rode my dick and the other took a ride on my face. My attention immediately locked in on Ty's clit, and I wasted no time sucking the delicate nub in between my lips and feasting on it. The sound of her moan was faint due to the kisses between her and Carrie, but I felt the vibrations rattling through her body, and that was what I was listening to. Carrie's pussy was tight, hot, and wetter than the bluest oceans of the world, making it hard for me to breathe under Tynesha's already steady rainfall. She knew that though, and it was always a battle to make each other cum first. The way that she was swirling her hips when she only had the head of me locked inside her walls made it clear that goal was to make me cum fast and hard. My hands shot out to grab Carrie's hips at the same time that I introduced my tongue to the party I was throwing at Ty's clit. The quick flickering of my tongue, combined with the firm grip that I had on Carrie in order for me to lift my hips and fuck her back, had both women moaning in sweet chorus. Ty's motion of grinding her pussy against my tongue increased in speed, which made me fuck Carrie that much faster and harder. We chased each other in an endless circle until we came together in a perfect harmonious symphony that had their passion filled screams echoing off of our bedroom walls. I drank from Ty's pussy like it was a popped champagne bottle, trying not to miss a drop of her gushing orgasm, as my own cum steadily pumped inside Carrie in a fierce battle with the hurricane her pussy was forecasting. After a few moments, Ty climbed off of my face, and Carrie intentionally leaned down to kiss and lick the residue off of my lips while creating a new seduction with her mouth. It was a few more moments before Carrie climbed off of the dick, standing beside Ty, wearing an identical triumphant expression.

"You-You think you've won, b-but I'mma get my lick back," I panted, feeling wonderfully and thoroughly used.

"You always say that, but it'll forever be two against one, so you might as well accept defeat," Carrie said, smiling devilishly while taking Ty's hand in hers.

"What she said," Ty added, laughing softly.

"Mark my words... I have not yet begun to fight you two," I replied.

"Oh, lawd, now he's quoting old, dead white people," Ty said.

"Pussy done sent him to another realm of reality," Carrie said, laughing.

Ty joined in her laughter while pulling her toward the master bathroom. Once the door closed behind them, I heard the shower turn on, but I made no move to get up from my prone position. It was actually my intent to drift back off to sleep, but just as I was nearing the land of blissful slumber. my ringing phone snatched me back to the present. I rolled over and grabbed it off of the nightstand, not recognizing the number, but knowing that it was coming from the States told me that it was gonna be some bullshit on the other end.

"Yeah?" I answered.

"Mr. Bishop, this is Raul calling from Ridge Crest. I was told to inform you that there was a situation outside of the institution a few hours ago."

"What type of incident?" I asked, sitting up and swinging my feet to the floor.

"There was an unknown vehicle sitting outside of the institution, and our security followed the strict instructions that you mandated."

I automatically knew what that meant because when I took over the institution and made the security additions, I'd made sure all the employees knew to shoot first and ask questions never. That was the price anyone paid for venturing onto private property uninvited. Instinctively, I'd known that once Royal and his family figured out that there was no legal way out for Tesha, they'd get desperate and go for what they knew. So, I'd made sure that everything was in place.

"Did anyone make entry?" I asked.

"No, sir. The facility remains secure, and all residents are accounted for."

"Good. Let the local authorities know so that a proper police report can be generated and keep me in the loop," I instructed.

"Yes, sir."

Once the call had been disconnected, I considered my options. I had local law enforcement on the payroll, and every security person was employed by my own private security firm that was based out of Ghana comprised of soldiers handpicked by General Udoku. It was a situation where I held all of the advantages, but one could never underestimate an opponent like the Walkers, and that was why it was good to try and anticipate their next move. I doubted that they would personally make a move on the facility if they knew what they were facing, but they weren't really in a position to ask the cartels for their help. The Juarez Cartel had double crossed them, the Sinaloa Cartel was still getting dope from me thanks to the pipeline my late Uncle Umar had opened for them, and the Zeta Cartel was run by their most hated enemy currently. There were other gangs, organizations, and criminal enterprises that the Walkers could align themselves with in order to storm the castle that I'd turned Ridge Crest into, but I wasn't really worried. In the event that someone did make it inside to rescue Tesha, my staff already knew to kill her quick.

After everything she'd done, there was no scenario in which she came out of that facility alive, and my conscience was very much clear with that decision. As a precaution, I sent an encrypted text to the head of the Sinaloa Cartel so that their soldiers could be on standby, and then, I sent a message to Carlito, who was the head of the Juarez Cartel, just in case anyone with the last name Walker crossed into Mexico. With that done, I got up and headed to the bathroom to piss. I opened the door to the sight of Ty and Carrie exchanging sounds of passion as they made love to each other under the water's pounding downpour. Immediately, I had the desire to join in. The sight of their gorgeous, naked bodies moving in sync like an underwater ballet had me stuck in one spot, staring for a moment, as slight jealousy filled me. Both women had thick curves and fat asses, but Carrie's titties were about a size bigger than Ty's. They worked out together in more ways than just sexual, so all traces of their pregnancies had evaporated months ago, leaving them with flat stomachs that would make a high school girl envious. I knew that I was a lucky nigga, and both women consistently made sure that I felt that way.

"David, are you coming?" Ty asked seductively.

As badly as I wanted to indulge, I knew that if I did, we'd more than likely spend the entire day fucking like wild rabbits, and no work would get done.

"You two finish without me, and I'll meet you downstairs," I replied.

No response came from either woman, only the increased sounds of passion that were sexy enough to test what little willpower I had left. I was able to refrain though as I took a piss and washed my hands before going back into the bedroom. I threw on a pair of gold silk pajama pants and made my way down to the kitchen where I put in a breakfast order for the three of us. When I was done with that, I went outside on the veranda.

"Hi, Daddy!" Dayjah said, running up to me with her arms wide open.

I scooped her up quick and gave her a smothering hug that made her laugh and squirm at the same time.

"Good morning, princess. How are you?"

"I'm fine, Daddy, just playing with Rashon, Rashawna, and Stormy. Auntie Fina let me help feed them after I ate breakfast."

"Thank you for being so helpful, sweetheart," I replied, putting her on her feet and following her over to where her siblings sat around, playing. They were less than a month away from their first birthday, and I'd already been told by my great aunts and uncles that a big celebration was planned in all of their honor. Dayjah was about two months away from turning six years old, and this would be the first birthday I was around to celebrate with her properly. I was looking forward to it more than she was because all she was worried about was getting the giraffe that she asked me for. I spent a few minutes just basking in the glory of my children until I felt a tap on my shoulder, and I turned to find my Aunt Zynefa with Deante in her arms. His smile was immediate and contagious as he reached his little chunky arms out toward me. He was only eight months old, but his intelligence was already apparent, just like his recognition of who his daddy was. As I pulled him into my arms, he immediately started jabbering away in his adorable baby talk.

"I just changed him after he was being his usual greedy self at breakfast, but you already know that he was straining his little neck looking for you since he woke up this morning," Zynefa said.

"I saw him from my window, looking around while everyone else was playing. Is this your way of telling me that I spoil him, Auntie?"

She gave me a knowing look that made me chuckle because we'd already had the conversation more than once about me spoiling my children. I understood that she wanted me to raise them with realistic expectations because the world wouldn't just throw rose petals at their feet, but those were lessons to be taught later in life. Right now, I just wanted the kids to enjoy being innocent and to give them the royal treatment that I didn't grow up with.

"No matter how much I spoil my children, I have faith that you, and the rest of the family, will help me to raise them to be grounded, respectful, kind, and generous human beings. Just like the rest of our family," I said.

"If only that were true."

Her comment caused me to take my eyes away from my smiling baby boy and look at her closer.

"What's that supposed to mean, Auntie?" I asked, studying her body language.

Her hesitation was obvious, but I knew that she would tell me what was on her mind because I was closer to her than anyone in the family.

"There has been... talk. Now that you live here permanently and you brought your family with you, there are others who feel like you're too American to be a true African king. They also blame you for your Uncle Umar's death."

None of what she said really surprised me because I'd seen the looks from some of my family and the soldiers under my command, but for her to say that the talk was more so open now was a problem. This was exactly how a mutiny started, and that threatened my entire family.

"Tell me how you feel about this 'talk', Auntie."

She took a furtive glance around before taking a small step closer to me.

"You were your Uncle Umar's favorite nephew and the rightful heir to the throne, but this belief made him unpopular with some. None who would speak a whisper while he was still alive because he wouldn't have hesitated to make an example out of anyone. Now that he's dead though... I fear that you have inherited some of his enemies, as well as made some of your own with everything that's happened within the last year. How Shaomi died shook a lot of people despite the respect they have now for Queen Tynesha. The fact that you live and openly fornicate with a white woman does make others question your ability to put your people and their needs above your desire to be politically correct by the American standards that you grew up with. If your uncle were here, he'd tell you to either grow some eyes in the back of your head or address the problem head on. You must remember that you're not an elected official like the American president. You're a king, a dictator, and that means showing force when necessary."

The look that she gave me made it clear that the situation that she was describing now was a time when I needed to show force because the rules of the jungle were simple. You either ate or you got eaten. Out of my peripheral vision, I saw Ty and Carrie come outside hand in hand, smiling like they didn't have a care in the world.

"Summon General Udoku and I want both of you to meet me in the war room," I demanded.

She nodded curtly and walked away just as Ty and Carrie made it to where I was standing. I could tell right away that Carrie only had eyes for Deante, but Ty was locked in on me.

"How's Mama's baby boy?" Carrie asked, holding her arms out.

Our son immediately started bouncing in my arms and squealing before he began reaching for her with all of his little might. I passed him to her, but my eyes never strayed from those of my wife, and she immediately stepped close enough for me to smell the sweet cocoa butter soap on her skin.

"What's wrong?" she asked.

"Nothing, I got it," I replied.

"What's wrong?" she asked again with more force in her tone.

Her tone caught Carrie's attention, and suddenly, I was looking at two sets of eyes who had the ability to see through my bullshit.

"Listen, there's a slight situation that I've gotta go address with Udoku and Zynefa, but I promise you both that there's nothing to worry about, and I can handle it. I just need you to remain here inside the compound until I return," I replied.

They briefly looked at each other before their eyes swung back to me, and I could see the questions about to leap from their lips like the sounds of passion they'd so recently shared. Thankfully, they kept their tongues at bay, and two servants stepped out onto the veranda carrying our breakfast.

"I ordered for us, but you two eat without me, and I'll be back soon," I said, kissing them both on the forehead before heading back inside.

I headed back upstairs and took a quick shower, trying to decide how I wanted to do things with this potentially lethal situation. Having my Aunt Zynefa by my side to dispense the wisdom my Uncle Umar would've given me helped me not to feel panicked or overwhelmed, and that made the solution I sought appear in my mind's eye. I finished my shower and then threw on a charcoal gray pinstripe Black Billionaire suit with matching gray Black Billionaire loafers. Once I was dressed, I headed to the war room that I kept on the north side of the mansion. When I walked in, both General Udoku and Aunt Zynefa stood up from their positions at the small conference table in the middle of the room.

"My king," Udoku said, bowing respectfully.

"Take a seat, both of you. I want us to handle this situation swiftly and decisively," I stated.

"What is the situation, and how would you like to handle it?" Udoku asked.

I nodded at my aunt, and she quickly explained to the general what she'd informed me of outside on the veranda. When she finished, his eyes came back to mine.

"My aunt will compile a list of names of those who have been 'talking', and I suspect that we'll be able to root out any more potential enemies that way," I said.

"And when we do, how do you want to deal with it, my king?" Udoku asked.

"The only way to deal with treason is death, and it must be a death that sends a message," I replied emotionlessly.

Chapter 3

(Tesha)

Before consciousness fully registered, my feet were on the floor, and I was up out of bed. At first, I didn't know what had awakened me from my Thorazine induced slumber, but then the faint sounds of gunfire reached my ears, and my mind cleared a little more. I knew that there was a chance that my mind was playing tricks on me because I was being held on the outskirts of nowhere, but my instincts told me that those were definitely gunshots ringing and singing. It didn't sound like a little gun going off either. A few seconds later, an alarm started blaring loudly outside my room in the hallway, which confirmed what I'd heard while giving me slight hope for what it all meant. I took a step toward the door, but it suddenly opened, and four white men in all black came in fast like a swarm of wasps.

"Please," I begged softly.

I never got the chance to say more before I was snatched up off of my feet by two men and forcefully slammed on my back on the bed. The next thing that I knew, I felt a prick on the inside of my left arm, and then a warm feeling spread throughout my body before I went limp on my way back into unconsciousness. From that point on, my nightmares began. It always started off with my baby girl happy and healthy in Royal's arms, but that image only lasted for a short period because the demon that was David showed up and brought hell with him. The worst part was the helplessness I felt because these nightmares were vivid enough to feel like I was actually there, but I couldn't do a muthafuckin thing. It reminded me of all the months that I'd been tormented in my sleep by nightmares of my twin sister, Tynesha, killing me or my child, but this was worse because of the hatred that I always envisioned in David's eyes.

There was no way for me to keep track of time, so it didn't surprise me that when I finally opened my eyes again, the room was awash with sunlight. The pain in my stomach instantly reminded me of how long it had been since my last meal, and the weakness that I felt throughout my entire body backed up that opinion. I laid there in bed for a few moments and tried to take stock of myself to see if I'd been hurt in any other way besides mentally. I kept expecting to get fucked up by the people working here based on the horror stories that I'd heard about these mental institutions, but so far, nothing too serious had happened. Some people actually liked me for killing a cop, even though technically, my twin had done it. Nobody fucked with me enough to get me out of this bitch though. There was video footage of Ty killing Roland, so it was pointless to deny that part. The thing that fucked me up was that there was no record in any database of us being twins. The lawyer that I'd had made sure to check everywhere, including the hospital that we were born in and the schools that we went to, but there was no record of Ty having a twin sister. There wasn't even any DNA samples *anywhere* to compare as proof that I wasn't her.

I'd been completely erased and left holding the bag for the things that Ty had done. I knew David and Carrie played a part in this setup, but this move was bigger than them. I didn't know who the fuck had helped to make me vanish, but in my heart, I knew that my husband and my in-laws wouldn't just leave me to rot in this place. I understood that this was where it paid to be part of the Walker clan. It took me about twenty minutes of staring at the ceiling before I felt steady enough to sit up, but I still made the movement slowly.

Once I was upright, I was able to see the clock, and the fact that it was three o'clock in the afternoon surprised the hell out of me. They'd hit me with a serious dose when they'd ran down on me this time, which made me wonder what happened with the shooting that I'd heard. One thing that I knew for sure was that I couldn't get any answers sitting in this room, so I slowly grabbed my stuff to take a shower and then ventured out into the hallway. There were other patients out moving around, but my eyes were on the two sentries posted at each end of the hallway. This was new as were the mini assault rifles in their grip. From what other patients had told me, security had never been this intense... until I arrived. That knowledge didn't flatter me. It added to my stress levels because I'd been trying to figure out a way to escape ever since I was arrested in Mexico. The extra time I'd almost gotten for my actions in the jail would've been welcome because I would've been in a more populated area with more people to potentially bribe. Ridge Crest was privately owned, and whoever owned it paid its employees well enough that they wouldn't consider doing something strange for some change. Or maybe I just hadn't found the right person.

I made my way to the shower, trying not to draw too much attention to myself, and I spent a half an hour scrubbing myself until I felt human again. This was the only moment of privacy that I got in here, and for that reason, it was in here under the water's downpour that I allowed my tears to fall.

The ache that I felt from being separated from my little girl was without definition or end and only rivaled by the hatred that I felt toward Ty and David for taking her from me. I'd always known that David would feel some type of way about me raising our daughter without him, but I never thought that he would've taken it this far. And the fact that

Ty helped him, once again betraying me, was a bigger knife twisting in my soul. I wasn't dumb to the fact that I'd betrayed her first by fucking her husband and getting pregnant by him, but my child was innocent, and Ty was ignoring the fact that removing me from her life was ultimately damaging her. I couldn't let that continue to happen, so I had no option except to find a way out of this hell. Once my tears had dried up for the moment, I got out of the shower and put my clothes on. When I stepped back into the hallway, the armed guards were still posted, but my attention went straight to the door to my room because it was open wider than I'd left it. I was bracing for the worst as I approached slowly, but then I saw the housekeeping cart parked just inside my room, and my paranoia lessened a little. It was standard protocol for someone to come around to each room daily and clean it up. It wasn't exactly hotel service, but it kept the administration from having to give the patients access to cleaning materials. When I walked into my room, I intended to put my shoes on and leave the room until the housekeeper was finished, but when I saw who was cleaning the room, I froze in place and dropped everything in my hands.

"Tell-Tell me I'm not hallucinating or still locked inside some sick, twisted ass nightmare," I said, feeling both hopeful and desperate.

"No illusions, bitch. I'm here," Nyaisha replied, opening her arms to me.

This was absolutely the last place I expected to see my crazy ass cousin from New York, but I stepped into her arms with palpable relief.

"Oh, my God, how did you get here?"

"I've been trying to keep tabs on shit ever since I went back up top to New York, but I got caught up in my own drama with my cheating ass baby daddy. By the time I tuned back in, all *hell* had broke loose. Your face was plastered on every news station for killing a cop way out here in Hang

Em High Texas, but when I tried to contact David and Tesha, I couldn't find them anywhere. So, I had to wait to see how shit was gonna shake out before I could make a move. Now, tell me what the fuck is going on, and how did David let this happen?" she asked.

"David didn't *let* it happen. He *made* it happen."

"Huh?" she asked, completely confused.

"Okay, first off, I'm Tesha, not Tynesha. It was Ty who killed that cop, but then her and David set me up to get caught for it in Mexico and tried here in Texas."

"Wait, so your twin set you up? That shit sounds crazy, cuz," she said, shaking her head in disbelief.

"There's so much bad blood between us that I don't even know where to begin the story. I know that you were in Florida with us, and we were all closer than a muthafucka, but my mom and I had been keeping David's secret. We'd both fucked him and were pregnant with his kids, so you can imagine how fucked up shit got once the truth was exposed."

"Ohhhh, fuck!" she exclaimed.

"Yeah, exactly. Shaomi was the one to expose that particular secret, and that pretty much opened the floodgates that destroyed our family. I was hurt, but for real, I didn't care because I married Royal Walker, who is the man of my dreams, and we'd started our life over in Russia with my daughter, Stormy. Then, I fucked up and let my paranoia get the best of me by thinking that Ty was gonna keep her promise to kill my daughter... So, Royal went to kill her and David for me. That was the beginning of the end for real," I said, shaking my head sadly.

"This shit is wayyy deeper than I thought, but regardless, we have to get you out of here."

"You got a plan?" I asked, hopeful.

"Nah, not exactly. Just getting this job was as far ahead as I thought, and I figured that I'd eventually be able to link up with David and his people to use their resources. I should've known that it wouldn't be that easy though because in reality, Davie Boy had the juice to get you out without my help."

"I've got more resources than David. All you have to do is get to my in-laws," I said confidently.

"I'll do you one better," she said, reaching into the pants pocket of her khaki uniform and pulling her phone out.

I was so happy that I could've kissed her, but instead, I snatched the phone and quickly dialed Royal's number. The insistent ringing on the other end lowered my hopes the longer that it went unanswered. It wasn't until I hung up and called back to get the same results that I finally admitted the truth. My love was still in a coma. Despite the immediate feeling of discouragement that accompanied this realization, I was still able to push through, and my next call was to Angel. I expected to hear her voice after a few rings, but it never got that far because my call went straight to voicemail. When I called Freedom and Destiny, I got the exact same results, and my hope evaporated like steam after the hot shower was over.

"Everybody's phone is turned off," I said dejectedly.

"When was the last time you talked to them or heard from them?"

"They used to communicate through my lawyer because they'd retained him, but I haven't heard anything from anyone since I got here a few months ago. From the moment that I got here, I felt so isolated and cut off from the world. It's like I'm dead and forgotten," I replied.

"I'd never forget you, cuz," she said, pulling me toward her and hugging me tightly again.

I fought the tears clogging my throat for a few seconds, but then they forced their way out, and I was left sobbing uncontrollably. Nyaisha didn't say anything; she just held me tighter because she knew that was what I really needed.

"What's going on here?"

The accusatory tone and the deep rumble of the voice that came from behind me caused both of us to jump and immediately separate.

"Nothing's going on. Just some girl shit. Do you mind?" Nyaisha asked with much attitude.

"There's no contact allowed between staff and patient," he said.

"Yo, you're just a security guard, so mind your fucking business," she replied.

The sound of him pulling the slide on what I knew was an assault rifle made me turn around and use my body to shield my cousin.

"This is all my fault, not hers. I just got emotional because I saw her, and her physical appearance reminded me of somebody I knew," I said, holding up my hands.

He didn't say anything at first, but the look in his eyes let me know just how little he cared about taking both of our lives. Despite that though, I was halfway convinced that I had him ready to disregard the whole thing until his eyes shifted away from mine and landed on the phone still in my grip. The words 'oh, fuck' were on the tip of my tongue, but I swallowed them in hopes of some type of miracle.

"Where did you get that?" he asked.

My first instinct was to play dumb, like I didn't know what he was talking about, but I knew that was sure to piss him off, and that was worse than a bad idea.

"You stole my phone," Nyaisha said, quickly snatching it from my grip in anger.

I still didn't say shit because my eyes were locked on his, and I could tell that he wasn't buying the shit that we were selling.

"Give me the phone," he demanded, holding one hand out.

"What? Give you my phone? You bugging, my dude, because we definitely don't know each other like that," she said.

"You claim that this patient stole it and that you didn't give it to her. Okay, so let me check your call log to see when your last call was placed because you're not supposed to have your personal phone inside the institution," he reasoned.

"Fuck that. You not my boss, and I don't gotta do none of that shit you talking bout. So, go ahead and report it, and it'll be my word against yours," she replied, not wavering in her boldness.

When he raised his AR-15 to shoulder height, I thought that it was just a scare tactic, but then I saw all of the emotion drain from his eyes, leaving only a glacier blue glare.

"Wait!" I said, attempting to take a step forward.

I never saw him pull the trigger, but I felt the heat of the bullet speed past my temple, and then my brain registered the sound of fast-moving metal piercing flesh and bone. When I quickly spun back around to face Nyaisha, I immediately saw why she didn't cry out or scream. The bullet had hit her smack in the forehead and lifted the front top of her skull off, exposing her pinkish gray brain matter.

"No," I whimpered.

Before I could move toward her body, I felt a powerful blow land squarely on the back of my head, and the next thing that I knew, I was lying right next to Nyaisha, fighting unconsciousness. I could feel the pounding of footsteps through the floor, no doubt signaling the response to a shot being fired in close quarters. My vision was swimming, but I could see well enough to know that the armed guard had pulled my cousin's phone from her pocket. I wanted to stop him, but the message that my brain was attempting to send to my body to compel it to move was getting lost in translation somehow.

"What happened in here?" I heard another male voice ask.

"Patient Bishop was trying to escape, and this housekeeper was assisting her."

"We were told to be on high alert for this... Grab Bishop and let's go brief the director," the man demanded.

My body still wasn't doing what I wanted it to, which only left me with the option of using my own voice to let it be known that I wasn't going any-muthafuckin-place. As soon as I opened my mouth though, the command of 'facility lockdown' started blaring over the intercom system nonstop. The next thing that I knew, I was hit in the head again, and everything went peacefully dark. Complete unconsciousness was my friend, but I didn't realize that until I woke up strapped down to a table in five-point restraints. I immediately knew that movement wasn't an option, even though I was still fighting the darkness lurking at the edges of my field of vision. I could hear people talking, and I chose to use all of my remaining energy to focus on what was being said. I recognized the voice of the man who'd killed Nyaisha in cold blood and knocked me out, but I didn't recognize the female that he was talking to. It was clear by the tone of the conversation who was in charge though.

"So, do we kill her or make her disappear?" he asked.

"I was told that it was up to my discretion but under no circumstances was she to remain here now that her family knows her exact location."

"So, what would you like me to do, Madam Director?" he asked.

"Right now, I want you to give her more of that tranquilizer while I decide. I'll render my decision on her fate within the hour."

Chapter 4

(Marta)

(Colombia)

"El jefa, the doctor is here to see you," Eduardo said, coming outside into the backyard where I was laid out by the in-ground pool.

"Show him in," I replied, not moving from my reclined position on the lounge chair.

Eduardo gave the instructions over his two-way phone, and a few moments later, the good doctor was escorted into my presence.

"Dr. Dracon, you're early," I said.

"One must never keep Jefa waiting. How are you feeling today?" he asked.

I waved my men away so that the doctor and I could have a private conversation, but I still didn't bother to sit up. When we were alone, I moved my feet to the side and indicated for him to take a seat.

"How do I feel? Alive, but it's bittersweet, so I'm hoping that you have some good news for me," I replied.

"Good news. Of-Of course. I would not want to disappoint you like my other colleagues."

I knew that he was referring to the fact that I'd killed his partner and all of his partner's family members, simply because he told me some shit I didn't like. In my defense though, I hadn't exactly been in my right frame of mind, but

I knew that I didn't have to remind Dr. Dracon of this. I just stared at him until I saw his forehead begin to perspire.

"Everything is going perfectly and according to plan, so you have nothing to worry about. I'll remind you that unnecessary stress is good for no one though, so I want you to try and remain in a positive frame of mind," he said.

"I bet you do. Sadly, stress is a part of my everyday life, Doc, and I don't see that changing anytime soon," I confessed.

"I understand, but I had to tell you that either way. Here are the results from the tests that you had me run. I triple checked everything."

He reached into his inside jacket pocket and removed a thick white envelope that he handed to me. I took it and slid it out of sight under my thigh.

"Thank you. Your payment will be forwarded, and I'll see you once I get back in town."

"Have you decided when you're gonna want me to perform the surgery on your heart to remove your little insurance policy now that you no longer need it?" he asked.

We both knew that I'd been gambling with life for the last six months by not having the bomb that connected my heartbeat to Royal's deactivated and removed. He could die from complications while in his coma at any moment, taking me with him, but it was the fact that his family would do anything to keep him alive that gave me confidence in the gamble that I was taking. The day that Royal had escaped had been the only time I was certain that I was gonna die, but as time passed, that fear had lessened. It hadn't evaporated, and my reasons for living were stronger, but I knew that Royal's family was still hunting for me. That meant the insurance was still necessary for the moment.

"We'll leave everything the same right now and talk about it in three months," I replied.

"Okay, Jefa. Buenos tardes."

I nodded as he got up and left me alone with my thoughts. That didn't last long though because Eduardo was back beside me in moments.

"What time will you be ready to depart, Jefa?"

"Get the plane ready while I change clothes," I replied, finally sitting up and rising from the lounge chair.

I made sure to grab the thick envelope that the doctor had given me and carry it with me as I headed back inside my mansion. I didn't really need the huge, fifteen-bedroom estate, but I was still the fearless leader of a cartel, and that came with status symbols requiring me to flaunt my wealth. I had to flex my power too. Coming back to Colombia with plenty of both hadn't just given me celebrity status. It had made me an instant legend outside of my father's name and legendary work. I'd never minded living in his shadow, despite his Mexican heritage, but I couldn't deny how good it felt to be my own woman in a game that was still heavily dominated by men. I knew that some saw the fact that Royal had escaped in Switzerland as a loss or a rookie mistake, but my rose-colored glasses saw things differently. My time with Royal had led to the forming of a powerful alliance that would soon put other criminal organizations and enterprises out of business. It was this knowledge and aforethought that was causing me to take the risk of leaving the security of my compound and venture back into the United States of America. I knew that there was a chance that Royal's father and sisters were somewhere on American soil because the word I'd received was that they'd left Mexico. They could've returned to Russia, but my instincts told me that they had no plans to go back there until they had my head to mount over somebody's fireplace. They'd be waiting for forever if that was their desire or goal. I quickly changed out of my bathing suit, exchanging it for some jeans and a thick sweater to go with my Michael Kors snow boots. The envelope that the doctor gave me went into my Birkin bag, and once I made sure that I had everything I needed, including my passport, I headed outside to the waiting Maybach truck idling. Eduardo slid on the back passenger seat next to me, and then the four SUV caravan moved out.

"The meeting with the other cartel leaders is set for two days from now, so we should have plenty of time to take care of business in the States before heading back across the border," Eduardo said.

"Did you take care of the transportation and make sure that it's completely bulletproof?" I asked, feeling my paranoia tugging at my subconscious.

"I did you one better. I bought an old transport plane for us to fly in, and our motorcade comes with us. We'll land in the U.S., drive to our destinations, and the plane will meet us back in Mexico City when we're ready to head to our next destination."

I nodded in silent approval of his move, thankful that one of the million problems before me was taken care of. Still, I sent silent prayers to Viktor and Paco for them to watch over me as I mentally prepared to stick my head in the lion's mouth.

It took us an hour to get to the airport, and by that time, I was ready for my afternoon nap. We quickly loaded up, and by the time we were taxiing for takeoff, I'd gotten comfortable in the backseat, and my eyes were barely open. The next thing I knew, sleep had claimed my soul, and I stayed that way until we landed in Colorado. By the time all of my SUVs had rolled off of the plane and onto the tarmac, there were a few different customs' agents waiting expectantly. I lowered my back window and motioned one over while digging inside my Birkin bag for my passport. When I handed it to him, he did a curious inspection, but it went as quick as I expected given my diplomatic status, courtesy of the Colombian government. The friends that I'd made in high places had been less than pleased about my untimely detention in Switzerland, so they'd made sure that it wouldn't happen again.

"And whom are you traveling with, ma'am?" the customs' agent asked.

"My personal security," I replied curtly.

He glanced inside of my truck before his eyes returned to my passport. After a moment, he walked away to confer with his colleagues, but I wasn't worried.

"We can take care of them in seconds, Jefa," Eduardo said confidently.

"That's not necessary. They're just doing their job."

It was less than two minutes later when the customs' agent returned, handed me my passport, and waved us through the opening gate that allowed us to exit. As we pulled off, I reached inside my bag and grabbed out my phone, and then I sent a text to the warden at ADX Florence to let him know that I would be at the prison within the hour. It wasn't until I wired him five million dollars that I received a thumbs up emoji to the message I'd sent. Greed was what flowed through American's veins, and that was the exact reason that loyalty was always for sale. It would be naïve to say that shit didn't exist and work that way the world over, but just as it was with slavery, North America had cornered the market on what it meant to be a 'fair weather' friend. For the right price, you could buy a man's firstborn, and he'd throw in the womb that carried that child just so he didn't have to share the money. I didn't mind this flaw in their design because I sought to exploit it at every possible turn. Five million dollars was a lot of money to the warden, but to me, it was a small price to pay for the freedom that I so desperately needed in my life. I spent the forty-five minutes it took for my Maybach motorcade to pull up at the prison sally port contemplating my next move after this one. What I had planned was sure to cause a fast-moving ripple effect because my dad had loyal supporters, and a war for power with the other cartels was imminent. I was more than prepared though.

"Do you want me to come inside?" Eduardo asked.

"No, I got this," I replied, climbing out of the truck into the biting cold weather.

By the time I got to the back gate, it was opening, and a heavyset white man was there to escort me. He didn't say shit, and I offered no salutation as I fell into step behind him. He led me inside the employee elevator, and we took the three-mile ride down into the mountain where some of the world's worse criminals called home. Once we reached the ground level, he took me to the visitation area where I sat in a booth, separated from my father/s side by twelve-inch-thick bulletproof glass. I mentally and emotionally braced for what was about to happen, despite knowing in my soul that there was really no way to prepare. I concentrated on my breathing for the five-minute wait before my father was led onto the other side and pushed into his seat. Despite there being a camera in the top righthand corner over his head that captured every inch of both sides of the visitation room, the guard still didn't leave us alone.

"Well, this is a pleasant surprise. Why didn't you tell me that you were coming, Marta?"

"Because I know that all of your communication is being monitored, so it wouldn't have been smart to telegraph my moves," I replied logically.

He nodded, but I could tell by the look in his eyes that he was studying me intently. It didn't unnerve me as it normally would, which was even more proof to me that I'd stepped into my own as a woman.

"Something about you is different, my daughter. It would appear that the last year is catching up with you."

I looked down for a second, but it wasn't out of shame or some sense of failure.

"It's part of my plan," I replied.

"Your plan to do what exactly? Replace what you lost or what was taken from you? Surely you know that even for someone who wields your power, this is impossible."

I shook my head sadly at the man sitting before me.

"The father that I remember, the one who raised me in his image later in my life when I needed him, didn't believe in the word impossible. It's obvious that this American prison has broken you beyond repair," I stated.

The way that his eyes narrowed on my face was meant to intimidate and inspire fear, but it no longer worked on me.

"Broken me? This coming from the little girl playing big boy games, all the while thinking with her pussy instead of the wealth of knowledge I gave you? I think it's clear which one of us is broken beyond repair," he replied, looking me up and down in disgust.

Both his statement and the look on his face made me laugh humorously.

"Why have I never noticed how closeminded you are until now? You're stuck in time that no longer exists in the real world outside of these walls you've been staring at, and you're clearly out of touch with reality."

"The reality is that my daughter isn't a leader of men like I taught her to be. She's just a woman that powerful men use as a cum dumpster and incubator," he stated maliciously.

I could feel the smile spread across my face as my eyes flickered toward the guard, and I gave him a subtle nod. He keyed his radio, without saying a word, and a few seconds later, the red light beside the camera's lenses, signaling that it was working, went completely dark.

"You sad, little man. You're too drunk on yourself to see that I'm the definition of power, and that power grows with every beat of my baby's heart," I said, placing my hand on my bulging stomach.

"How does being knocked up with another bastard child make you any more powerful than the last time? You couldn't even protect that child into adulthood."

"Simple. This child that you call a bastard is fathered by Royal Walker, and not even you are so far out of touch that you forgot how powerful the Walker family is. I'm carrying their next generation, and I'm on the brink of uniting the most feared cartels in Mexico, who will follow me like a god as they pray to my son like the new Messiah," I replied, smiling triumphantly.

"You will *never* unite the cartels! Especially not after I snatch back control with one phone call," he said, smiling like he'd won.

I looked at the guard again and gave him another subtle nod. In the blink of an eye, he had a fistful of my father's hair, exposing his throat, and then he swiftly sliced open his main artery. The look of utter shock on my father's face as he tried in vain to catch the fast-moving blood gushing in between his fingers gave me a feeling of satisfaction that I hadn't felt since Royal's dick was spasming inside my pussy. I stood up and pressed my face to the window, needing to see all of the life drain from his eyes. The feeling of my son kicking inside me seemed oddly poetic, and my hands went back to my stomach as the last bit of color drained from my father's face.

"Adiós," I said, blowing him a kiss before I turned and walked away.

It took me ten minutes to get back outside of the prison and back behind the tinted windows of my truck.

"Did it go according to plan?" Eduardo asked as we pulled away.

"More or less but the look on his face was even better than I could've imagined."

"Do you want me to make the next move?" he asked.

I nodded while looking out of the window at the snowcapped mountains in the distance. I heard him pull his phone out and make the call that would get the heads of the Sinaloa and Juarez cartels' leadership decapitated. Those heads would then be put on display outside of one of my properties in Mexico City. When news of my father's murder in prison spread, it would reinforce the loyalty that his followers had for me, and the moves that I'd made against our ops would inspire terror all across Mexico. This was what the Americans called a hostile takeover. If all went according to plan, then by the time we crossed back into Mexico, I would be the new reigning queen, more formidable than Griselda Blanco. All that would be left was to unit my kingdom with the one that my son's father was born into. As Royal's firstborn son, my baby was the bridge that would create something like a nuclear power in the underworld, and the effects of that would be felt worldwide.

Now, it was time to bring Fathergod and the rest of Royal's family up to speed because their forced alliance had just turned into family. What had started out as just business had definitely become more than personal. Not in their wildest dreams would they expect me to be coming to dinner.

Chapter 5

(Fathergod)

(Russia, Three Days Later)

"Dad, you need to eat something," Free said.

"Get out," I replied, lifting my glass of tequila to my lips and taking a healthy gulp.

"But Dad, you haven't eaten in days, and you need…"

The look that I turned on her froze the words in her throat, and she slowly, wisely, backed out of the dimly lit bedroom that I'd commandeered inside of Royal's castle. In my heart, I knew that my oldest daughter was just trying to help in an impossible situation, but I didn't want her help. I didn't want anyone's help to grieve the loss of another child. I just needed to shed enough blood to fill the Atlantic and Pacific oceans. That was how I wanted to grieve. I'd done my duty as a father yesterday and made sure that my baby was properly laid to rest in her own Russian monument, but I'd buried my heart with her. I was beyond consoling, and I'd said just as much to everyone when I'd distanced myself from my entire family. I'd spent the last day sipping different liquors, never feeling drunk enough, existing with the shadows in my chosen bedroom as even darker thoughts played on a loop in my mind. There were times when I could still feel Destiny's blood on my hands from the hours that I'd held her body after her soul had long escaped to a higher plane of existence. Something inside me knew that there was nothing in this world that would cleanse that feeling of blood, and so I accepted it as my pentagram to carry into hell with me.

I didn't care, just so long as I got to take a lot of people to hell with me. The sound of the bedroom door creaking open again made me want to reach for my gun now, but the face that came into my line of sight banished the thought while making my heart hurt even more.

"Daddy," Truth said, coming in the room toward me until she was able to climb up into my lap.

I knew that I smelled like a distillery full of liquor, but my baby girl didn't care as she laid her little head on my chest and got comfortable. I was a gangsta who'd long ago learned the art of not just suppressing my emotions but shutting them off, and yet I could feel the tears sliding soundlessly down my cheeks. Before Truth had been born, Destiny had been my youngest daughter, and the memories of her in this exact spot made my heart hurt. The pressure of the knowledge that I'd failed my daughter was a crushing weight, leaving me lost because everything that I'd believed about myself was proven false. Destiny hadn't died because of a decision she'd made. It was my call to run down on that facility without a carefully formulated plan, and that had cost a price that I'd never wanted to pay. That was the thing about death though. It didn't offer refunds or exchanges. As badly as I wanted Destiny back, not even my willingness to give my own life for hers was a deal that God or the devil could honor. I heard Truth take a deep, relaxing breath, and I immediately knew that she was moments away from falling asleep.

I looked down at her, and she looked so precious. This had become her pattern since she was a baby, and normally, it warmed my heart beyond measure, but right now, I felt completely undeserving of the unconditional love and faith that my still innocent child was giving me. The longer that I held her, the more the warmth of her love worked to thaw my hardened heart, but it still wasn't like it used to be. I wasn't who I used to be, and right now, I had no idea who I was outside of being a coldblooded murderer. Movement in front of me caught my eye, and I looked up to find Madeline standing just inside the doorway. She didn't say anything, and truthfully, we hadn't spoken since I'd arrived back in Russia. Neither of us knew what to say to each other, but to me, that was better than the hollow words of condolences we could've been slinging back-and-forth.

I knew that Madeline had come to love Destiny just like she had the rest of my kids, so I knew that she was in pain over her loss. I didn't know if she blamed me, but she would've been perfectly right to because she had told me not to take the violent approach to getting Tesha back. If I would've listened to her, or at least taken that moment to contact her before making a move on the facility, then Destiny would still be alive. With that unspoken truth between my wife and I, there was really nothing that could be said. Everything that had happened was my fault.

"I can put her in her bed if you want," Madeline offered.

"No, she's okay."

"Hmm... so, Truth is the only person that you can stand to be around?" she asked.

"She's the only one who still sees me as a hero... but I'm sure that in time, I'll do something to erase that illusion along with her innocence," I replied, taking another drink of tequila.

For a second, Madeline just stared at me, but then she crossed the room to stand beside me, and she removed the glass from my hand. She tossed the remaining liquor down her throat before sitting the glass on the nightstand and perching on the arm of the chair that me and our daughter were occupying.

"I couldn't have loved Destiny anymore if I'd pushed her from my own womb, so I want you to know that I'm feeling your pain. We all are, including Destiny's daughter, who doesn't really understand why her mommy had to go live in Heaven. It's okay to feel that pain, Jonathan. It's okay to grieve, and because I know you so well, I'm gonna tell you that it's understandable for you to feel guilt. What's not okay is this one-man pity party that you've been throwing. That's not the man that I know and married."

"I don't know what you expect me to say or do," I said, working to control my anger and not direct it at her.

"I don't really want you to say anything, Jonathan. We lost a daughter though, and we're still on the verge of losing another daughter if we don't get Tesha back, so I want you to do something about that. I want Destiny's death to mean something, and I promise you that it won't mean a goddamn thing if you give up and lose yourself inside of a liquor bottle."

Her tone wasn't harsh, but her words cut like a sharpened barber's straight razor. One of the things that I'd always loved about Madeline was her lack of fear when it came to me, and she'd shown that even when I was a notorious prisoner under her authority at Guantanamo Bay. There was no fear in her, but there was more love and compassion than I deserved in a thousand lifetimes together with her. When I looked up into her eyes, it was those emotions that I saw, not a hint of guilt or a shadow of judgement. The feeling of Truth's little hand pulling on my shirt made me look down, but it was clear to see that she was already fast asleep and dreaming peacefully. From somewhere deep inside me, I found this to be inspiring because I knew it was my job to protect my baby's peace and preserve her innocence for as long as possible.

"Uh, Dad. You need to come downstairs," Angel said.

When I looked up to find her standing in the bedroom doorway, I immediately saw the barely contained fury contorting her beautiful features, and it struck the chord of my protective instincts.

"What's wrong?" I asked, passing Truth to Madeline as I stood up.

"You have an unexpected visitor," Angel replied.

"Who?" I asked warily.

"The Red Devil,' she replied.

"Marta is *here*?" Madeline asked, sounding almost as shocked as I felt.

"Who captured her?" I asked.

"No one captured her. She showed up at the front gate and demanded to see you," Angel replied.

"Oh, shit... That must mean that the rumors are true," Madeline said softly.

When I turned my quizzical gaze on my wife, I could tell that she definitely had some information that she needed to share, but we'd get to that later.

"Take me to her," I demanded, following Angel out of the room.

As she led the way downstairs, I pulled the AR-15 pistol with the forty-round clip from my shoulder holster and pulled the slide to chamber a .762 round. Angel led me to the library, and when we pushed through the double doors, I saw the guns of Lil Boy, Big Baby, Bone, and Free all trained on Marta's head. She appeared unfazed though as she reclined on the couch, but as I approached, I quickly realized why.

"Don't think for a second that I'm above shooting a pregnant bitch," I said venomously while pointing my pistol at her attractive face.

"If the legend of you is even half true, then I have no doubt that under normal circumstances, you wouldn't hesitate to splatter me, or my unborn son, all over this beautiful sofa. Of course, by now, I'm sure that you know these *aren't* normal circumstances," Marta said.

"If you think that bartering with my son's life is a smarter move, or one that guarantees your safety, then you're still underestimating my capacity for ruthlessness," I said, increasing the pressure of my finger on the gun's trigger.

"I'd never underestimate the Almighty Fathergod nor would I gamble with my child's life. I lost a son at the hands of your son, Royal, so it's a pain that I know intimately and one I never wish to experience again," she stated, staring at me with surprising sincerity.

For a second, my resolve wavered with distraction, and I actually weighed the consequences of killing this woman right here, right now. Destiny's grave wasn't even cold yet, so there was no way that I could put Royal in the plot next to hers so soon simply because I couldn't control myself. I was better than that.

"What-the fuck-do you want?" I asked in a low growl through clenched teeth.

"It's simple. I wish to permanently unite our families and pursue complete control of criminal enterprise on a global scale," Marta replied seriously.

"Is this what they mean by the craziness of pregnancy brain?" Angel asked.

"Nah, this is some dumb shit on a different level," Free commented.

Typically, I would've agreed with Free, but something in Marta's eyes told me that her tone was serious because she actually believed in what she said.

"So, let me guess. All we gotta do is break your dear old dad out of prison," I said dryly.

"No, that won't be necessary," she replied shortly.

"There's no way that you could join up with us or anyone else without your father's approval because you're only running shit while he's away," Free said.

"I think she found a way around that – permanently," Madeline said, coming into the library and crossing the room to stand beside me.

It wasn't until my wife put her hand on my arm and pushed it downward to force me to lower my gun that I looked over at her.

"What are you doing?" I asked.

"I think that you might want to hear her out because my sources say that her father was murdered in prison... while she was there, supposedly to visit him," Madeline replied.

When I looked back at Marta, she had a mischievous smile on her face and a deadly twinkle in her eyes. She wasn't trying to hide the truth from me because she wanted me to know that she'd had the balls to assassinate her own father. I found it mildly interesting.

"Okay, so now you're the semipermanent leader of the Zeta Cartel, at least until someone knocks your head off," I said, unfazed.

"Maybe... or maybe I'm more than what you think I am," Marta stated calmly.

"Bitch, quit playing before I air your ass out my damn self," Free threatened.

"Hold up, Free. I think that I know what she's talking about," Madeline said.

"I'd wager that it has something to do with the chatter we've been hearing about the war reaching a boiling point in Mexico," Bone said, looking at Free.

The look that they exchanged was one of clear understanding, but it did nothing for me because I didn't know what the fuck they were talking about.

"One of you fill me in on what I missed," I demanded impatiently.

"The Sinaloa Cartel and the Juarez Cartel both lost their leadership within the last forty-eight hours. Taken out by lower ranking members close to them. The strange part of it is that there hasn't been a power struggle or even a power vacuum. It's like everyone has fallen in line under new leadership," Madeline explained.

When my eyes narrowed on Marta's face, she actually laughed out loud, and I could see just how much she was enjoying her coupé.

"That don't make sense. Okay, so you killed your father, who was one of the most powerful men in Mexico, but that's not enough to make those other cartels follow you. What's the catch?" I asked.

For a long moment, Marta didn't speak. She just stared at me in an openly curious evaluation.

"Your son is very much like you, and maybe that is what has made it harder to hate him even when I know that I should. No matter now though because we are all one big happy family. To answer your question, the 'catch', as you put it, is the considerable force of nature that is your family. Believe me when I tell you that the cartels don't want the problems that you can bring, especially given your Russian allies," Marta replied.

"So, you think that because your life is linked to Royal's through the bomb that you've had put on his heart that we'll back your play to conquer Mexico?" Free asked, scoffing sarcastically.

"No. I think you'll back me because nothing means more than family," Marta replied, reaching into her bag slowly and pulling out a thick white envelope.

Her gaze stayed locked on mine as she extended the envelope, and after a moment's hesitation, I took it and opened it. No sooner had I read the first line involving DNA testing did all the pieces finally fit together, and I shook my head at the sheer diabolical genius of this bitch. I read the papers in silence, and then I passed them to Madeline.

"Bullshit," she muttered a few seconds later.

"I'd like to say the same, but something tells me that the Red Devil wouldn't step to a real demon with a lie. Not to mention that it makes a twisted kind of sense," I said.

"What's going on?" Free asked.

"She's claiming that baby she's carrying is Royal's," Madeline said, passing the paperwork to Free.

"And how the fuck would that make any kind of sense?" Angel asked.

"Because Royal killed her son, so in her mind. she owed him a life, and she probably knew that Tynesha wouldn't deliver Stormy. It explains why she kept him and released Ty, all while sending everyone on an impossible prison break mission. She needed time, and she had all of her bases covered," I replied, begrudgingly respecting the strategy of it all.

"So, wait, you turkey basted yourself a bastard child by my little brother?" Free asked, taking a menacing step toward Marta.

"No turkey baster needed, trust me. We fucked... A lot actually. The rest is self-explanatory," Marta replied nonchalantly.

It was on the tip of my tongue to say that he'd never do that to Tesha, but I kept my mouth shut because my brain was busy calculating all the advantages.

"So, what is it that you want right now? Why are you here?" I asked, refocusing on the imminent threat that Marta still posed.

"Well, originally, I was coming to deliver the news in person, seeing as how you probably wouldn't have believed me any other way. When I heard about you losing your daughter though... I wanted to offer my condolences and any help," she replied.

"Help? Help how?" Angel asked.

Marta didn't answer verbally, but she was staring at me intently enough for me to understand. She came with an army close enough to strike back at my enemies. That meant that she was now my righthand of vengeance.

Chapter 6

(David)

(Three Days Previous)

I looked around the room slowly, making sure to level my most judgmental gaze on the thirteen people gathered around the conference table I was sitting at the head of. The group of people was a diverse mixture of extended family members and soldiers who'd once been under my Uncle Umar's command. The stench of blood was heavy in the air due to the torture that each individual had been made to endure, but I felt absolutely no remorse for the actions taken. It was too important to root out all the traitors and potential traitors, so feeling remorse for removing an eyeball with a dull spoon or clipping a nigga's nuts was a luxury that I couldn't afford. Truthfully speaking, I didn't wanna feel remorse or guilt, which was why I kept reminding myself that they'd brought it on themselves. The sight of General Udoku entering the room focused my thoughts on what needed to happen next.

"Sorry for the delay, my king, but I'm happy to report that each person's name that was provided has been rounded up, and now we simply await your orders," Udoku said.

I nodded at him. and he took a step back against the wall so that I could address everyone at the table. I pulled out my pistol as I stood up, and suddenly, the chill of death could be felt caressing the air.

"I trusted all of you, and this is why it breaks my heart that we've come to this place now. The American side of me that each of you has criticized secretly wants to show you compassion and give you all another chance to be loyal to me and my régime. However, I find myself asking what my Uncle Umar would do. Undoubtedly, he'd remind you all that there's a difference between compassion and weakness," I said, raising my gun.

Without further delay, I shot three men in the face. When people started scrambling out of their chairs and running toward the door, Udoku and his men pulled their guns out and shot them down. In less than sixty seconds, everyone held captive had been executed, and their blood was soaking into the carpet beneath my booted feet.

"I want every man and woman here to be taken to the nearest town, and I want their bodies to be put on display for all those who would dare conspire against me to see," I instructed.

"It will be done, my king," Udoku replied.

I surveyed the carnage for a few more moments before stepping over and around bodies on my way out of the room. Once I made it outside, I took several deep breaths in an attempt to steady my mind in preparation for the talk I knew I'd have to have with Carrie and Tynesha. This little light massacre had taken place away from the main house, but I had no doubt that the gunshots had been heard. I felt like I needed a shower before anything else though, which was why I headed back to the house and snuck up the back stairs to my bedroom. After stripping out of my bloody clothing and walking into the bathroom, I stepped under the hot water and tried to fight against the shivering in my body that I could feel resonating up from my soul. I'd killed people before, but this whole situation had a different feel to it. I could justify it as protecting my immediate family from a serious potential threat, but the fact that it had been an all-out slaughter was something that my conscience couldn't ignore. If this was what it meant to be a dictator, then maybe I wasn't the king that my people needed. When I heard the shower door open behind me, I looked over my shoulder to see Ty's naked body through the steam heading toward mine. Neither of us spoke, and I didn't resist when she turned me toward her and pulled me into her arms. After a few moments, the shaking in my core became less pronounced, which told me that the chill of death had passed. I held onto Ty for what seemed like a long time, still not speaking, but she wasn't rushing me in any way. The love that I felt for her was astonishing to me, especially after all the shit that we'd been through and put each other through. Our journey up to this point would've destroyed anyone else, but somehow, we hadn't crumbled. We'd come out stronger on the other side.

"I feel like my Uncle Umar would be ashamed of me," I said softly.

"No, he wouldn't. He'd understand and know that whatever you did was because it had to be done. Umar had no doubts about you, David. Him and I first talked about all that would be expected of you when you were saving his life in Miami and got shot for it. That situation showed him just how tough you were mentally and emotionally, and he knew that you'd have to be both in order to be the great king you were destined to become."

"But is this what I'm destined to be? I'm out here killing people just for questioning my ability to be king," I said, shaking my head.

"The people have a right to their opinion, but there's a difference between that and planting seeds of doubt. You know like I do that a seed of doubt will grow into a vine that chokes the shit out of us, so I know that you understand that you did what you had to do. Don't question that."

I considered her words, choosing to hear the truth in what she spoke instead of continuing to feed my own doubt.

"I love you," I said sincerely.

The way that she smiled up at me was beauty personified, and it made me pull her close to me as I sought her mouth with my own. I kissed her slowly, tenderly, yet passionately until the heat from the hot water was drawing warmth from us. I picked her up and then sat down with her right under the water's downpour. It felt like a torrential rain when I slid my dick up inside, but her throbbing pussy was the perfect port to shelter us in this storm. She rode me ever so slowly as we continued kissing like we were each other's snorkel under water. It had been a while since we'd made love like this, but it felt like what I needed right now, and I gave myself fully to the moment. The passion forced the pressure to build fast, and the grip that her pussy was putting on me had me fighting my need to cum all inside her every time she rose and fell. She rode my dick like she was on rails, slowing winding her hips like a rollercoaster going through a rolling turn. I was losing myself so fast inside of Ty that I didn't realize we weren't alone until I heard someone clear their throat with purpose. I looked up to find Carrie standing there with the shower door open, but the look in her eyes wasn't one of lust.

"What's wrong?" I asked immediately.

My question caused Ty to look over her shoulder in Carrie's direction, but her hips kept moving with purpose.

"Your phone rung, so I answered it. There was another incident at the facility in Texas," Carrie replied.

"We'll be right there," Ty said, turning back to me and riding my dick faster.

"They said it's important," Carrie stated.

"So-So is this," Ty panted.

I was helpless to offer up any words of protest or argument because my eyes were already rolling into the back of my head. I was barely conscious of Carrie closing the shower door before my climax ripped through me to connect to Ty's orgasm, putting a paralyzing hold on her.

"Shit," she grunted, collapsing against me.

I laid down on the floor of the shower until our hearts started to beat normally again as I waited for my brain to return to the necessary functioning needed to address whatever the fuck was happening in Texas.

"Hop up, bae, and let's go see what the problem is," I said, squeezing her ass cheeks gently.

"That's not a very romantic afterglow, but I get it," she replied, slowly rising and taking a step back so that I could get up.

"That definitely reminded me of our early Orlando days," I said, pulling her back into my arms and kissing her again softly.

"Mmmhmmm, when shit was simpler."

"Best week ever," I whispered against her mouth while running my hands up and down her body suggestively.

"If you start with me, we're gonna be in here a lot longer," she warned, smiling.

I didn't mind that, but I knew that another call from Ridge Crest wasn't a situation that I needed to ignore. Reluctantly, I put a hold on the seduction, and we both quickly washed each other's bodies. When we came out of the shower and back into the bedroom, we were greeted by Carrie, who was sitting on the bed with my phone in her hand. Ty went to put on some clothes, but I walked straight over to Carrie with my dick swinging and stood in front of her naked, holding my hand out for my phone. She willingly handed it over, but her eyes didn't move up above my waist. I placed the call back, and as soon as I was informed about what happened, my desire for more sex was put on hold as I sat next to Carrie on the bed. My mind immediately began to consider how Ty was gonna feel because she loved her cousin, Nyaisha, as much, if not more, as her twin had.

"The patient is to be transferred immediately. Get her to my safehouse in Atlanta, Georgia in case another attack is planned, and I'll send the plane immediately," I instructed.

Once the directive that I'd given was repeated back to me for confirmation, I hung up the phone and sighed heavily.

"What's wrong?" Carrie asked.

"We had an unexpected loss," I replied.

"What does that mean?" Ty asked, coming out of the walk-in closet.

When I looked at her, I couldn't automatically find the words, but in the end, I decided on the direct approach.

"Nyaisha tried to break Tesha out of Ridge Crest... And the security did what they're paid to do," I replied.

I saw as the shock initially registered on Ty's face, and then tears clouded her eyes.

"So, you're saying that they killed Tesha or..."

Her question trailed off, and the pain that I felt for her made me take her hand and pull her onto my lap. I'd fucked with Nyaisha for real, and she wasn't a part of my beef with Tesha, so I hated that she died because of it. The collateral damage was starting to pile up surrounding the decisions that I'd made, and I needed to find a way to minimize that moving forward.

"I'm sorry, sweetheart," I said sincerely, wiping the tears from her eyes.

Carrie reached over and gave Ty's hand a gentle squeeze meant to offer comfort, but she didn't say anything.

"Just tell me that Tesha's bitch ass ain't get out," Ty said.

"No, she didn't. I just gave the order to have her moved to Atlanta until the plane gets there because it's obvious that despite the new security measures, the institution is not as impenetrable as I wanted," I replied.

"Where do you want to send her?" Carrie asked, taking my phone back from me and texting instructions.

"Bring her here," Ty said.

"What?" I asked, looking her in the eyes.

The sadness of losing her cousin was still evident, but the determination in her hazel green eyes was what I was focused on.

"This needs to end, David. I know that we were all in agreement on making her suffer for the rest of her life, but as long as she's alive, she's a threat. It might've been

Nyaisha that ended up getting to her, but we know how resourceful Royal's family is, and none of us is naïve enough to think that they're just gonna forget about her. She pledged her loyalty to them anyway, so we need to take her out of the equation," Ty stated in a matter-of-fact tone.

"Are you really willing to kill your sister?" Carrie asked.

I knew the answer to that question even before her mouth opened to respond, but I felt like Carrie was asking because part of her believed that her and Ty had grown too close to hurt each other. Maybe that was something she needed to believe in order to feel like part of our family now, but she obviously hadn't realized how much Ty had changed in the last year and a half.

"You damn right I'mma kill her disloyal ass, and I won't feel no type of way about it," Ty stated emphatically.

"David?" Carrie asked, looking toward me for some type of reasoning.

"What do you want me to say? Tesha brought this shit on herself, and Carrie, you know this because we actually went to see her when she was in jail to offer her an olive branch. She more or less spit in our face and told us to go straight to hell. She made her bed," I replied.

"Exactly. And I'mma provide that turndown service for her ho ass. Get her here, David," Ty demanded, storming from the room.

For a second, I had the urge to go after her because I felt like she needed me to console her, but I knew if she was serious about Tesha dying, then she was gonna be too busy psyching herself up to hear anything rational. So, instead, I went and threw on a white linen suit with a pair of matching Gucci loafers while mentally preparing for the next moves to be made. When I came out of the closet, Carrie was still sitting in the same spot with my phone in her hand and a far off look on her face.

"You okay?" I asked.

"Not really," she replied honestly.

I sat beside her on the bed and took one of her hands in mine.

"Talk to me, sweetheart."

"Is it crazy that I feel like Ty is gonna kill me too one day?" she asked, looking at me with more than a hint of fear in her eyes.

"You know that I'm not gonna let that happen. Plus, you're a big part of this family."

"David, that sounds good, but she's about to mastermind the murder of her twin, the woman that she shared a womb with, so it's obvious that being family don't mean I get to keep breathing," she reasoned.

"Them sharing a womb makes them related, but it's only the loyalty that truly makes a family. At the end of the day, you have my loyalty... and my love," I said, leaning in to kiss her softly on the lips.

She gave me a bright smile despite the worry swirling in her brown eyes.

"I love you too, David... And for that reason, I need to know that I can trust you with a secret right now. It has to stay between you and I and not even Tynesha can know."

"This sounds more than a little serious," I replied hesitantly.

"It definitely is."

"Okay, well, talk to me," I said, feeling suddenly concerned.

The cautious look that she threw over her shoulder only added fuel to my belief that whatever she was about to confide in me was deadly serious.

"I'm pregnant," she whispered.

I could feel the wide smile spread across my face as I pulled her in for a big hug.

"I thought that your pussy felt wetter than usual."

"David, this isn't a time for jokes because something tells me that when Ty finds out, she's not gonna celebrate with us," she said.

"Of course, she'll celebrate and be happy with us. You're just being overly paranoid because of the way she's carrying shit with Tesha. You're not Tesha."

"You're right. I'm not Tesha. I'm not Shaomi either, but the common theme of your wife executing your baby mamas is justified fuel for my paranoia. Not to mention the fact that Ty hasn't gotten pregnant again by you since that unfortunate miscarriage, and I know she's been trying, which is why her sexual appetite has picked up. I feel like if either of us tells her that I'm pregnant before she gets pregnant again, or before she calms the fuck down a lot, then she's gonna find an excuse to kill me. To be real muthafuckin clear though, David, I will *not* just let her kill me or our kid, and I'm not about to let her take me from our other son either," she said adamantly.

"I'm not gonna let anything happen to you or our kids. I promise," I replied, cupping her face in my hands and staring her in the eyes so that she could see my determination.

I understood the doubt staring back at me, but I knew that Carrie trusted me with hers and our son's lives, which was why we were talking right now.

"I got you," I vowed.

"You better. Because I'm telling you right the fuck now that if I feel any type of bad vibe from her, I won't hesitate to use a .223 bullet to change her mind. Permanently."

Chapter 7

(Tesha)
(Three Days Later)

As much as I'd partied with drugs and alcohol, I would've sworn that I'd experienced every level of high, but whatever I was being shot up with had me so high that I didn't ever want another drug in my system. I just wanted to get off of this ride so that the world would stop spinning like a fast amusement park ride. I had no idea where I was or how I'd gotten here, but each time I'd gained some type of coherent thought, I could tell that I was in a different environment. One time, I could've sworn that I was on a plane. For the longest time, I wasn't restrained, but the drugs had my arms and legs as useless as a limp dick in a whorehouse. Now that I was feeling like enough of my strength had returned for me to try and run for my life, I could feel the bite of handcuffs into the flesh of my wrists. I opened my eyes to find myself cuffed to a hospital bed, and there was an IV drip hanging above me. At first, I was trying to understand or remember what the fuck had landed me in the hospital, but then I realized that the hospital bed was actually inside of a regular bedroom. The room was as unfamiliar as having the IV drip inserted into my arm, but at least it wasn't some mental facility. At least that was my initial thought, but with each second that my mind was allowed to clear, the question of where I was became a more pressing one. Something about this place felt vaguely familiar, but my brain wasn't moving fast enough to catch the thread that was running away from me when I tried to make shit make sense.

"Well, good morning, Sleeping Beauty. It's great to see you again."

The familiarity of her voice inspired both hate and fear in equal measure, yet there was still part of me that hoped I was hallucinating or having an all too familiar nightmare. When she came into view, it felt like I was seeing her in 4D extra high definition, and she was definitely real.

"Wh-Where am I?" I asked weakly.

"Um, I'd say that you're in hell, but because I ain't killed you yet, I guess this would be the in between place considered purgatory. You should recognize it though," Ty replied, smiling maliciously.

Only the tiniest part of me wanted to believe that my twin wouldn't kill me, but the truth of the monster that she'd become was all too apparent.

"So, you broke me out, just to kill me? That was mighty white of you."

"Broke you out? Baby, my husband owns the facility that you were in, so getting you from there to here was nothing more than a phone call," she bragged.

"If your husband owns that facility, then you're just as much to blame as he is for what happened to Nyaisha. Our mother is rolling over in her grave right now because of how fucked up and heartless you've become."

"Fuck you, bitch! Don't try to put that on me because you're the one who pulled Nyaisha into this situation," she raged.

"Nah, sis, that was your doing too. Nyaisha didn't know that you'd tricked me into your position for killing that cop and left me to rot while you erased all traces of me. She was there to rescue you, not because I called her but because she was loyal to you and couldn't understand how anyone would just leave you locked up in a mental hospital," I said.

I could see the immediate denial ready to fly from her beautiful lips, but the obviousness of the truth froze her, and for the first time in a while, I caught a glimpse of my sister. The realization of the truth paralyzed the features on her face, making it obvious that it hadn't dawned on her that *she* was the actual cause of our favorite cousin dying. There was absolutely no part of me that felt bad for her, but antagonizing her served me no good, so I didn't say anything else. The ensuing silence said it all and then some. A figure came into the room behind her, but I couldn't tell who it was until he got closer.

"Bae, why are you doing this to yourself right now?" David asked, walking up behind Ty and wrapping his arms around her.

The display of simple affection made me want to vomit as I questioned whatever I had seen in this man that would make me disgrace my body by fucking him multiple times. At this point, I'd rather die than have him fuck me.

"You're right. I'll deal with this bitch later," Ty replied, stepping out of his embrace and leaving the room.

I knew that my spoken truth had gotten to her because she didn't say shit to me or even look me in my face. Her departure left me and David alone in a room together for the first time in a long time.

"So, you were the wizard in the nightmare version of Oz that was Ridge Crest? I should've figured," I said with disdain.

"If you're expecting me to feel bad for you, I'm sorry, but that ain't gonna happen."

"I have no illusions about the heartless bastard that you've become too, Your Highness," I replied.

"Yep, I'm as heartless as you were when you kept my daughter away from me. In case you were ever trying to figure out how you ended up in this situation, it was the decision that *you* made to keep the child that *we* created away from me."

"Can you really blame me, David? Everybody around you was dying or getting shot, not to mention the attempted car bomb. Stormy wasn't safe around you with the growing list of enemies you had, so keeping her away from you was me being a good mom and keeping her safe. Or did you forget that your *wife* vowed to kill our child?" I asked.

"I ain't forget shit, but it's obvious that you did because your version of events is definitely a rewrite of the historical events designed to make your choices seem righteous. Allow me to refresh your memory. I didn't have any enemies in Orlando until a certain nigga named Roland was brought into the mix. Granted, he was Ty's ex, but you were his fucking flunky, which makes you just as responsible. And let us not forget that you were right there in the thick of the bullshit when Ty and I went to war with that nigga in the streets of Miami and Orlando, which made us all enemies of Zoe Pound. You remember Viktor Bah, right? Or maybe you remember his wife and daughter that you and Ty tortured while I was laid up in the hospital fighting for my life. It seems like you have selected amnesia about who had enemies hunting for them, but the difference is that we didn't marry into a powerful family and try to hide like your scary ass did. Which brings me to my last point. I could live another hundred years and never have as many enemies as the Walker family, so in what world would *my* daughter be safer as one of them?" he asked, clearly angry.

My mind had been coming up with justifications as he'd been going on his tirade, but none of that shit would've mattered because the ugly truth was that he was making valid points.

"Even if you're right, you still didn't have to erase my fucking existence and lock me in a crazy asylum."

"You're right. I didn't have to, but I was being merciful. What I should've done is gave you to my Uncle Umar's soldiers and let them decide your fate. You remember my Uncle Umar, don't you? The one that you betrayed and murdered, even though he'd only ever showed you kindness and loyalty?" he asked, taking a menacing step toward me as his tone dropped low enough to send chills down my spine.

"I didn't-I didn't mean for that to happen," I stammered.

"It don't matter what the fuck you meant because dead is still dead, and you still have to answer for that."

"But you can't kill me. I'm Stormy's mother, and she needs me," I replied, fighting the cracking in my voice.

"Needs you? My daughter don't need you when she has an entire country willing to lay down their lives for her without hesitation, and their loyalty will never be in question the way that yours always is. Stormy won't even remember you."

"Don't do this," I begged.

"It's crazy because I could've sworn that I told you something along the same lines when I begged you to let me see my daughter after she was born. I don't recall you showing me any mercy, so give me one good reason why I should show you any."

I didn't open my mouth or try to respond in any way because I knew that we were beyond whatever bullshit lie I could try and spin. Appealing to his empathy wouldn't get me shit either, which left me no way out.

"Cat got your tongue?" he asked, smiling maliciously.

"Fuck you, David!"

"We definitely already did the fuck out of that, and I'll pass on any idea you had about running it back. Sorry, you'll have to settle for Royal's dick being the last one that you'll ever have."

"You know what will happen to you if you do anything to me, right? You know just how ruthless the Walker family is, and I'm one of them now, so I'm untouchable," I said, smiling with false bravado.

He looked around the room for dramatic effect before his eyes came back to mine.

"I don't see them here to save you right now."

"They don't need to be, but you know that eventually, they'll figure out what you had to do with all of this, and then they'll be on your muthafuckin ass," I replied with growing anger and confidence.

"I don't know what part of your delusional little mind thinks that I'm scared of the Walkers or give any fucks about what they'll do, but you're obviously still high as giraffe's pussy. You're talking about a 'family' going up against a king, and the math ain't mathing, sweetheart."

"David, it doesn't have to be like this. We're much more powerful and profitable if we work together, and I know that math makes sense to you because you're about your money," I said, attempting to take a reasonable approach.

"Damn, you must really be desperate if the only move that you have left is to appeal to my greed. I can appreciate the sentiment, but I'm doing alright by myself," he replied, wearing a smirk on his face that made me wish that I could shoot him right-the-fuck-now. Instead of focusing on that impossibility, I focused on what else I could do or say to prevent the inevitable. I couldn't think of a single thing or person that was gonna save my life, which left me sending silent prayers to a god that I hadn't communed with since my younger years.

"Will you at least grant me a last wish?" I asked as tears filled my eyes.

"You can ask, but that don't mean I'mma give you a muthafuckin thing."

"Can I see my daughter please?" I begged shamelessly.

For a split second, I saw a flash of mercy in his eyes, but it vanished so fast that it might've been an illusion or just my projection of hope. When he suddenly turned around and left the room, I knew for sure that any trace of humanity that I had thought remained inside of David was nothing more than a figment of my imagination. Alone in this room, condemned to die sooner or later, I had to admit that I'd played my hand all wrong. Getting pregnant by David had been a happy accident but making an enemy of him had become my fatal flaw. Deep down, I knew that I was smarter and more calculating than that, but somewhere along the way, I'd lost my edge. As much as I loved my husband, I understood that my falling in love with him had changed and transformed me in a way that was my gift and my curse. The ability to put my full trust, my heart and soul, and ultimately my life in the hands of that one man had given me comfort and peace. It had also dulled my razor-sharp instincts of knowing how to play the angles. Making Tynesha my enemy was dumb enough on my part, but then intentionally alienating the one muthafucka who could rebuild a bridge between her and I, while keeping me safe, was just beyond stupid. The fact that I'd been unwilling or unable to see that shit until this very moment only made me sadder.

"How the fuck did I get here?" I wondered out loud.

"Sometimes I ask myself that same question.'

I looked up to find Carrie standing just inside the doorway.

"What-What are you doing here?" I asked, surprised by her presence.

"I live here."

Her declaration caused me to look around the room in reevaluation because there was no reason that Carrie's house should've been familiar to me. There was also no reason there should've been this many African artifacts in her house, but really looking around helped me to understand the feeling of familiarity I'd experienced when regaining consciousness. This was David's home in Ghana, which I'd attempted to take by force once upon a time.

"You live here... with David and Tynesha? How does that work?" I asked, more than a little curious.

"It's a long story that's not important to your current situation. Is there nothing that you can say or do to prevent Ty from killing you?" she asked, crossing the room toward me.

Her question was a logical one, but the intensity and concern that I could feel behind it was out of place.

"Why do you seem so concerned, Carrie?"

She didn't offer up any kind of explanation, which only tickled my instincts more.

"You've always been closer to Ty than you were to me, so that would mean that your loyalty lies with her... and yet I sense something off within your question. Since I'm gonna die anyway, you might as well tell me because it's guaranteed to go to the grave," I said.

"I just don't think you need to die."

"Okay... and?" I questioned because there was definitely more.

"And Ty is making David's baby mamas disappear one by one. First, Shaomi. And now, you. And..."

The way her voice trailed off made my eyes widen as my mind tried to absorb the double barrel shot that I was reeling from.

"So, Shaomi is dead... and you have a baby with David," I replied, speaking slowly.

The way that her hand unconsciously went to her stomach was reminiscent because I'd been there, and it was very telling.

"The situation is complicated."

"You think? Well, let me give you some free game. If Ty killed Shaomi, and we both know what's about to happen to me, then you can bet your pussy that your ass is most definitely next. Just as soon as your baby is born, the clock starts," I warned.

'This will be our second child together," she blurted out.

I felt my eyes get bigger with shock, but I never got the opportunity to say anything.

"What are you doing in here?" David asked from behind Carrie.

When she turned to face him, my heart came to a skidding halt in my chest as I caught sight of my precious daughter in his arms.

"I-I was just talking to her," Carrie mumbled, sounding guilty of a major sin.

He looked at her hard for a moment, but then he moved past her and brought Stormy over to me. I could only reach for her with one arm, but he put her right on my chest, and the sight of her smile made the tears pour from my eyes. Everything in me wanted to stay alive for my baby girl and find some way to remove her from the clutches of the devil hovering over us right now. Stormy put her little chubby hands on my face and started speaking to me in nonstop gibberish that made me laugh as more tears poured down my face.

"My sweet girl, I've missed you so much," I sobbed, kissing her chunky cheeks.

The sound of her laughter broke my heart while warming my soul at the same time.

"Say your goodbyes," David demanded.

"David, don't," Carrie said.

The sudden fear in her tone was what caused me to pull my eyes away from my daughter and look up at her father. The chrome Smith & Wesson 1911 .45 seemed to shine brighter through my tear-streaked vision, but it didn't frighten me.

"You're not gonna shoot me in front of our daughter," I said confidently while holding onto Stormy tighter.

"Don't play with me, Tesha," he stated.

"David, just wait, there has to be another way to fix this," Carrie pleaded.

"Carrie, you need to leave the room. Now," he demanded, raising the pistol and pointing it at my face.

"Carrie, he's not gonna do it. We're family," I said, staring down the barrel of the gun.

"We are family, but I guess you forgot what that means. For All Mine, I'll Lay Yours," David said calmly.

I opened my mouth to respond, but the sight of fire leaping from the gun's barrel ended my speech. And then the bullet ended my thoughts.

Chapter 8

(Marta)

"How long would it take you to mobilize your people?" Fathergod asked.

"It depends on what we're doing and where we're going," I replied.

"I want you to make a move on a facility in Texas," he replied.

"I assume that you're referring to the place that you were at when your daughter was killed. What kind of move do you wanna make?" I asked, gauging the amount of destruction he desired.

"Royal's wife is trapped inside there, so I want her out of there first and foremost, and then I want that muthafucka levelled to the bedrock," he said with cold calculation lacing his words.

I knew better than to ask about saving anyone else inside of the building, so instead, I pulled out my phone and texted my lieutenant with instructions on what needed to happen. Within a few minutes, I received a response that put a smile on my face because it felt amazing to be the queen on the throne. I was officially out of my father's shadow. I could feel everyone's eyes on me, none more powerful than Fathergod's, but instead of providing a verbal update, I decided to just pass him my phone. I watched as he read the message of compliance and action before passing me my phone back.

"Dad, you're not really about to trust this bitch, are you?" Free asked.

I took no offense on the tone in which she asked it, but I did keep a close eye on Fathergod because I knew that he was a man that said more through silence than actual words. Our eyes locked, and I felt the understanding that somewhere in the back of his mind, he was already anticipating my very violent death should the slightest thing go wrong. I knew that it wasn't a threat; it was a guarantee, and the raw power that he emitted made my pussy sing like an old Mexican love song that made me smirk.

"Trust her? No, I don't trust her, and she's smart enough not to trust any of us. We'll use each other though," he stated in a calm but decidedly firm tone.

I could feel that nobody in the room was happy about the budding agreement, but what Fathergod said was law in this family. In all my years, I'd never known a man of such immense power until his very own son had wandered into my web.

"What is it that you want, Marta?" Madeline asked.

"I thought that I made that clear," I replied, switching my focus to her.

"You did when you were addressing my husband. I'm a woman though, and I know that you didn't stick your head in this lion's mouth for a business proposition that you could've easily made on your terms, in your territory. So, what is it that you want on a personal level because this is *far* from just business," she said.

My respect for her intuition made me understand that she was just as formidable as her life partner, which made their union make sense beyond the physical chemistry that swirled around them. It was obvious that she was no dummy, so my best move was to level with her.

"I need to see Royal," I confessed.

"Why do you say that like our very married brother was your sneaky link when you know damn well that he was your captive?" Angel asked disdainfully.

"I say that like a woman who's having a baby by a man that I respect, who wants that man to be a part of his child's life. RJ needs his father, and he shouldn't be punished for the decisions that his father and I made. Regardless of anyone's judgement," I replied patiently.

"RJ?" Free asked, giving me a quizzical look.

"Of course Royal's first son will be a junior," I stated, like it should've been everyone's forgone conclusion.

Looks were exchanged around the room, and my guess was that everyone was contemplating how Royal's precious wife would take this news when it was delivered to her. I didn't really give a fuck because she didn't have a choice but to accept the inevitable.

"I'm sure you're aware that Royal is still in a coma due to your adventures in Switzerland," Madeline said.

I could hear the judgement and blame in her words, which lined up with the tension and hatred I'd felt from the moment that I'd entered this house. To me, it was just background noise though, and I chose to ignore it.

"I've done some research on coma patients, and I know that they can hear you on some level when you talk to them. I'm speaking for me and my son, and I want to be the one to tell Royal that he has another reason to live," I said.

"Fuck no, bitch, you're the one who tried to kill him!" Free growled menacingly.

"Make no mistake, if I wanted Royal dead, then he would've been because he was all alone in enemy territory. Where was all of this protective energy then though? I mean, for such a loyal and righteous family, I've been wondering how it was that he ended up literally on my doorstep alone and unprotected in a country known for our savage treatment of outsiders. I can certainly own my part in Royal's predicament, but there's definitely enough room for blame to go around," I said, looking each person in the eyes.

The temperature of the tension rose immediately, and I could feel everyone's desire to kill me, but I knew that no one would move. My statement wasn't meant to flaunt this knowledge. It was only stated because these were the facts that needed to be understood so that people would stop looking at me from such a moral high ground. I'd definitely capitalized on everyone's mistakes, but they were still their mistakes.

"Since she's not leaving this house before holding up to the first part of our newly minted business relationship, there's no harm in her seeing Royal," Fathergod replied.

"I'll get a room ready for her to stay in. Girls, come help me," Madeline said, nodding to Angel and Free.

I could tell by their hesitation that they'd prefer to just shoot me and be done with it, but instead, they reluctantly went with Madeline out of the library.

"Come on," Fathergod demanded, nodding his head, indicating that I needed to follow him.

He led the way out of the library and across the hall to a private room that had been converted into a state-of-the-art makeshift hospital. Royal was laid in a hospital bed that was far from standard because it looked extremely comfortable and had enough buttons on it to resemble a space shuttle dashboard. In the corner sat a petite, Black girl in nurse's scrubs, reading a book. Her eyes lifted in casual inspection of who had entered the room, and then she went right back to the pages of her make believe. She looked to be in her late twenties to early thirties, so I was surprised that her face wasn't glued to her phone like the rest of her generation would be.

"How is he?" Fathergod asked, crossing the room to stand by Royal's bedside.

"Comfortable, but there's been no change. Some eye movement behind his eyelids, and his heart rate climbed briefly, but it only lasted for a moment before going back to normal," she reported.

The thickness of her Russian accent surprised me because I didn't know any Black Russians, but the world was definitely more diverse than I'd given it credit for in my youth.

"This is Marta, and she's gonna sit with him for a while. If she does anything, and I do mean *anything,* to harm my son in any way, I want you to shoot her in the head. Do you understand?" he asked.

I'd heard what he'd said, but the words didn't register until I saw her sit the book calmly in her lap and pull a .44 Ruger from under her right leg.

"Da. I understand," she replied.

When I searched her eyes, I found that the pale brown of them held a lifelessness that I recognized as the 'it factor' of a tried-and-true killer. I shouldn't have been surprised because there was no limit to how far Fathergod would go to protect his firstborn son at this point, but a gun totting nurse was different.

"I'll be on my best behavior. I swear on my son," I said, placing both of my hands on my stomach to emphasize my words.

He turned and looked at me hard for a few moments, and then he walked past me out of the room as if I were nothing more than a ghost.

"Tough crowd," I mumbled.

"Consider yourself lucky because normally nobody except for family is allowed inside this room. It's obvious that Mr. Walker doesn't like you or trust you, so I'm surprised that you made it this far," she replied.

"You're the hired help, so I could give a fuck what you think or what surprises you. You have no idea who I am or what I'm capable of, which is why I advise you to sit in your corner and shut the fuck up."

My words caused her jaw to flex instantly, and the finger on her gun hand slid inside of the trigger guard to rest on the trigger. My stare didn't wavier in the slightest, and it was definitely taunting her to raise the gun at her own risk. After a brief staring contest, I felt like I'd made my point, so I shifted my attention back to Royal, and I took a seat beside his bed. For a few seconds, I just stared at him as my mind filled with the moments that we'd spent together and the actions that had led to this point. The fact that this man had killed my first son and my son's father weren't things that I could forget, but every time I felt my unborn son kick inside of me, I knew that I redefined 'complicated' for better or worse. I knew just how much fight Royal had inside of him, so to see him so much thinner and smaller made him look more out of place.

I took his hand in mine and whispered a short prayer in Spanish for his soul to be protected in the unknown fight that he was locked in. It felt weird to speak to God about keeping someone safe I'd vowed to destroy, but I quickly remembered that destruction came in many forms. I wasn't delusional enough to think that Royal and I would have the typical coparenting relationship, but I knew that it would be his naïve, willful spirit that would make him believe that he could actually walk away from his firstborn. Undoubtedly, he didn't wanna have a baby with me, and I'd known that he'd wanted to remain faithful to his wife, but the reality of truth that him and I shared was that he'd secretly liked slutting me out. That secret pleasure would turn into massive guilt if he tried to abandon his son. Before that could be addressed though, he needed to wake the hell up.

"I know that it's gonna sound crazy to you, but I never intended for this to happen to you, Royal. I admit that I've been completely selfish when it came to putting my wants and needs before yours, but I never wanted you to be in a coma or dead," I said softly.

I could see and feel his private nurse watching me from the corner, but I kept my attention focused on him while ignoring the growing desire to remove her face from her skull with a spoon.

"I have much to update you on. While you've been on vacation for the last six months, I've been working overtime to secure a future that I could control. Despite you and I having some extremely complicated differences, I know that because of the cloth you're cut from, you wouldn't be able to deny the genius of my strategy. I assassinated the Mexican cartel leaders for Sinaloa and Juarez, and I had my father murdered too, so now all three cartels are under my command," I said proudly, smiling brightly.

The gasp that came from his nurse finally caused my eyes to shift to her for a second, and I could tell by the expression of shock on her face just how severely she'd misjudged me. On the outside, she only saw a beautiful Mexican/Colombian woman, extremely pregnant and soft spoken, but now, I knew that she saw the demon in my eyes.

"Don't they teach you not to judge a book by its cover in this part of the world?" I asked innocently.

Her mouth opened and closed twice, resembling a fish, but not a single word passed her lips, and so I turned my attention back to Royal.

"So, now I'm a queen with a whole queendom that our son will one day inherit, but he's gonna need your guidance to mold him into the man and leader he needs to be in order to assume his birthright. For that to happen, you need to wake up, and I've brought you some incentive," I said, giving his hand a gentle squeeze before letting it go.

When I reached in my pocket, the nurse reacted immediately by jumping to her feet and upping the pistol.

"Keep your hands where I can see them," she demanded.

"Relax, puta, I'm just grabbing my phone," I said, moving slowly and holding it up for her to see once I had it out.

A sheepish look covered her face, causing her to lower the gun, but she didn't sit back down. It took great effort for me not to get up and snap her pretty little neck, and the only thing that kept me in my seat was the more pressing issue of Royal. I quickly scrolled through my phone in search of a specific audio file, and once I had it, I played it out loud while holding the phone close to his ear.

"You hear that, Royal? That's your son's heartbeat. I need you to hear this and know that he needs you more than whatever is keeping you where you are. Come back to him," I said softly, taking his hand in mine again.

I laid my phone on his pillow and just let the strong pounding of our son's lifeforce echo throughout the room. When I looked up at Royal's nurse, I was surprised to see her face contorted with emotions of awe and sympathy, but I didn't comment on it. When she finally sat back down, I took it as a sign that she was finally beginning to grasp the concept that I wasn't there to hurt anyone, least of all Royal. For fifteen minutes, we sat there with the only sounds in the room being the machines that Royal was hooked up to and Royal Junior's heartbeat.

"What is that sound?" Fathergod asked when he came back into the room a few minutes later.

"What does it sound like?" I countered.

"Little girl, you really think that I won't shoot your silly ass in the face, don't you? Or have you failed to realize that there are fates in life worse than death?"

"I'm well versed in the art of torture, but that's a conversation for another day and time. I'm assuming that the sound you're referring to is this," I replied, moving my phone from Royal's pillow and extending it toward his father.

It took him a moment to really realize what it was that he was hearing, but I could tell when he figured it out because a surprised expression that was so uncharacteristic popped up on his face.

"Is-Is that?"

"Your grandson's heartbeat? Yeah, that's exactly what it is. I recorded it, hoping that one day I'd be able to share it with Royal so that he wouldn't feel like he missed anything," I said sincerely.

I could tell by the way that Fathergod looked at me that he didn't quite know what to say, which I knew was completely abnormal for him.

"This baby won't save your life," he warned.

"That's not why I'm here and trust me when I tell you that I can take care of myself," I replied.

"I guess we'll see about that, but just to be clear, when this reaches the point of you becoming expendable, I wholeheartedly intend to murder you in a gruesome fashion," he declared, smiling.

"I wouldn't expect less, but you'd be wise not to underestimate me," I replied calmly.

"Uh, sir," the nurse said.

"Are you threatening me, Marta?" he asked softly.

"Take it how you want," I said.

"Sir," the nurse said.

"You don't wanna play with me, Marta, because…"

"Sir!"

The urgency in the nurse's voice made both of us look over at her, and it was then that I realized that I'd been feeling pressure on my hand, like Royal was trying to pull away. When I looked at him, his eyes were open, and they were locked on me.

Chapter 9

(Fathergod)

"Get the fuck away from my son," I demanded, moving swiftly to his bedside.

If she hadn't been pregnant, I probably would've mushed her ass to the ground, but then again, if she wasn't pregnant, she undoubtedly would've ceased to breathe on the front steps when she showed up. I could tell by the look of utter confusion in Royal's eyes that he didn't know where he was or what the fuck was going on. The last thing that I wanted was for him to panic and think that this psycho bitch still had him held hostage.

"Stay calm, son, you're okay," I assured him, positioning myself between her and him so that I was all that he could focus on. Once recognition lit his eyes up, I could see the desire to speak, but I held my hands up to prevent that.

"Just hold on, son. We need to remove your feeding tube before you try talking. Sabrinna, how long will it take you to get that tube out of him?" I asked, giving the nurse a look to let her know just how impatient I was feeling.

"I-I don't know. I have to do it slowly and gently so that I don't fuck anything up inside of him. I need to concentrate," she replied, looking pointedly from me to the woman behind me.

"Point taken. Son, I need you to stay calm, and I'll be back in a little while. I'm not leaving. I'm gonna go round up the family and give Sabrinna space to check you out. Okay?"

He nodded slowly, but I still felt like I could read his mind, and he wanted to know what the fuck the Red Devil was doing under his roof. I turned around while strategically using my body to shield Royal from seeing Marta's big stomach as I pulled her toward the bedroom door. Surprisingly, she didn't resist or put up any fight. In fact, she didn't say a word until we were back in the library.

"You know that you can't hide me forever, right?" she asked, turning to face me.

For a brief moment, I allowed myself to envision the fantasy of shoving her into an oil drum and then submerging it in the earth like a time capsule. I could feel the smile stretching across my face, and I could tell by the way her eyes narrowed that she had some idea of what I was thinking.

"If I die, so does your son and grandson. Can you live with that... Fathergod?"

"I've never had the affliction that some people call a conscience, so why don't you ask me that again?" I said, pulling my Sig Sauer .45 out and placing it against her forehead.

At first, her features froze, and then she smiled in a sinister way that was damn near courting death.

"Jonathan," Madeline called out.

I looked up to see her standing a few feet away with Angel and Free on either side of her. I didn't see judgement in any of their eyes, but still I knew that this wasn't the move that I needed to make right now. I pulled the gun down and tucked it back in the holster under my arm.

"Royal is awake," I said.

"What?!" all of them exclaimed in surprise.

"Sabrinna is checking him over and removing his feeding tube, and then we'll go in and see him," I said.

"He woke up? Just like that?" Madeline asked, looking at me closely.

I knew that she could see the secret jealousy that I was trying to swallow because of Marta seemingly being the catalyst to bring my son back to us, despite the countless hours we'd all spent at his bedside.

"Dad... what aren't you saying?" Free asked.

I could feel Marta's flaming stare, but I knew that if I looked at her then I was gonna do some dumb shit for real.

"I don't know exactly what woke him up because I was arguing with this silly ass bitch," I replied, nodding toward Marta but still not looking at her.

I could feel my oldest daughter wanting to question me further, but she displayed her wisdom by keeping her mouth closed.

"You really don't wanna tell them what brought their precious Royal back into the land of the living? Or is it that you don't wanna tell them *who* brought him back?" Marta asked, sounding positively gleeful.

I tried closing my eyes and counting to ten, but I only made it to three before my eyes popped back open, and my look of death was fixated on Marta. Before I could say a word, Madeline was by my side, pulling my arm and taking me out of reach of the target of my fury. As badly as I wanted to resist my wife and simply give in to the urge to wax this bitch's muthafuckin ass on some after school shit, I refused to let Madeline see me get to that point. When I looked down into my wife's loving eyes, I found understanding there, and it eased some of the pressure in my chest.

"Unless you're trying to go into premature labor, bitch, I'd strongly suggest that you stop trying to play in my pop's face," Free warned.

I could tell by her tone that my daughter was as close to killing this bitch as I was, and that kinda repressed my feelings to do the same because I knew the guilt that she felt for killing people close to her siblings in the past. None of us would ever love Marta, but she was pregnant with Royal's first biological child, and that baby was our bloodline. That meant we'd tolerate this inconvenience for right now.

"Free, don't focus on her. With Royal being awake, we know that his move is gonna be to go after Tesha once he finds out she's gone, so we need to anticipate that," I said.

"The only way that I see him staying his ass in this house to fully recover is if *you* keep him here while we go to Texas and bring her back," Angel said.

"You can retrieve her from Mexico because my people have instructions to get in, do damage, and get back across the border," Marta said.

"And what's the timeframe on that action?" I asked.

"I don't know exactly," Marta replied.

"So, call your people then," Free demanded impatiently.

I expected Marta to fire off some smart ass response before pulling her phone out, but instead, her eyes found the Persian rug under her feet suddenly fascinating. At first, I just thought that she was being a stubborn muthafucka as usual, but then, a wild idea hit me.

"Where's your phone, Marta?" I asked.

The way that she cut her eyes at me told me that my thoughts were right on the money.

"What's going on, bae?" Madeline asked, sensing something.

"When I came back in the room to check on Marta and Royal, she was playing a recording of the baby's heartbeat through her phone out loud for him to hear. I managed to get her out of the room before he could see her stomach though. I didn't wanna overwhelm him or upset him so soon," I replied, still staring at the sneaky ass bitch avoiding my gaze.

"And you think that she left her phone in the room with Royal," Madeline surmised, nodding in understanding.

"Is that what woke him up?" Angel asked.

I refused to answer that question, but the smirk on Marta's face said it all, and it fed my anger some more. Instead of unleashing it on her though, I turned and headed back to his room to rectify the problem. When I walked in, I couldn't see Royal's upper body because Sabrinna was standing over him, but I could see that the feeding tube was out and lying on the bed next to him. My eyes went to the chair that Marta had been sitting in, hoping to spot the phone there, but it wasn't there. When I stood still and just listened, I didn't hear the racing sounds of the baby's heartbeat, which I thought was a good sign because that meant that Royal wasn't listening to it. But then I heard the chime of an incoming text message. The sound came from Royal's bed, which immediately drew me toward it. As soon as I got to a point where I could see around Sabrinna though, I knew that it was too late because Marta's phone was definitely in his hands.

"Royal, what are you doing?" I asked cautiously.

He looked up at me, and the hollowed look in his eyes had a haunting effect that caused concern to fill my chest where my oxygen used to be.

"Where's Tesha?" he countered.

"She's not here," I replied evasively.

"Dad... where is my wife that the Mexican cartel would have to break her out? And why the *fuck* would you be working with the Red Devil?"

His voice was weak and had a graveled sound to it like the rapper Pop Smoke, but there was still a force behind his words that reminded me of how strong willed he could be.

"It's a long story, son, but the short version is that Tesha got framed for murder and ended up locked in a mental institution in Texas. We're working to get her out now," I said.

"And the Red Devil is helping? I just read a text from her lieutenant saying that they'd be crossing the border with the package by sunrise. Why would you ever work with her after all that she did?"

"It's more than complicated, son, but you don't need to worry about any of that right now because I'm handling everything," I replied soothingly.

"Dad, stop trying to handle me and just tell me what the fuck is going on because there's no reason that someone as powerful as you has run out of resources to the point that Marta was your only option."

As badly as I wanted to protect him from the ugly truth, I knew that he was too much like me to be spun. The only approach that he would respect was for me to rip the bandage off.

"I need you to leave us alone for a moment, Sabrinna," I said, sighing as I sat in the seat that Marta had occupied.

She complied immediately, and once she was gone, I knew that it was time to cut through the bullshit.

"Look, son, while you were in a coma, there's been a war fought on many different fronts. David had Tynesha kidnap Stormy, and she's been taken to Ghana where David had a DNA test done to verify that he's her father. She's now officially considered royalty over there. While we've been trying to find a way to get her back, we were working on getting Tesha out, but when we made a move on the facility, we weren't prepared and... and Destiny paid the cost."

"What do you mean Dee paid the cost?" he asked softly.

All I could do was look him in the eyes, and after a moment, he nodded in understanding while swiping angrily at the tears that had escaped from him.

"That just happened a few days ago, and we've been trying to process the loss, but then Marta showed up on your doorstep."

"Showed up? You mean she actually came here of her own free will, and none of you splattered her shit?" he asked, becoming angrier.

"She's pregnant, Royal... with your kid."

I could tell by the way that his eyes closed and his head hit the pillow behind him that this revelation came with the force of a .223 round at close contact. I had no idea what to say because I didn't know what he was experiencing emotionally. My callousness came from years of hard living, and even though my son and been through his fair amount of bullshit for such a young man, I didn't wanna impart my negative views onto him. In my world, the ops died, no matter what, so even if it were my baby, I had a hard time believing that I wouldn't shoot Marta in her fucking face. What Royal decided to do would be up to him though because those were his demons to live with.

"Are you sure that she's pregnant?" he asked softly.

"She's big as a house, but we can run more DNA…"

"Nah, it ain't necessary. This was what she wanted all along because she said that I owed her a life. At first, I refused to fuck her, but in the end… I don't know, Pop. Part of me did feel bad for killing her son because he didn't have shit to do with the whole situation. What's crazy is that David tried to explain that to me on the night that we ran down on her house in Florida, but I refused to listen because what I knew was that one day that innocent little boy would grow into a vengeful grown man. I couldn't risk the danger in him coming to get his lick back," he said, opening his eyes and looking to me for understanding, not absolution.

The torment that he tried to hide in his eyes put a weight on my chest because I knew that directly and indirectly, I'd helped to create the parts in him that he was now questioning.

"Son, listen, I never wanted this for you or your sisters, but it's the life that comes with power from the legend that we've all created. There's nothing that we can do to unring any of the bells of the past, so those ghosts will continue to haunt. Once you can accept that, then maybe you can be the one to break the generational curses that your mother and I have passed down, and you can be a better father to your son."

"My-My son?" he asked, looking at me closely.

"Yeah, she's having a boy, and she's already calling him RJ, which means he's your junior."

He absorbed this information with a straight face, but there was the faint hint of a smile tugging at the corners of his mouth.

"It's okay to be happy about the innocent life that is about to enter this world, just remember to protect that innocence," I said gently.

"I know, Pop... It's just so much more than complicated. I don't know how to begin to explain this shit to Tesha, especially after all of the shit that David put her through."

"Let's just focus on getting her back, and then we..."

My comment was interrupted by Marta's phone pinging again, and I watched Royal glance down to read the message. The way that his chiseled jaw swiftly tightened reminded me of myself, and I knew that whatever it was wasn't good.

"What is it?" I asked.

"Go get Marta."

I had more questions, but I kept them at bay as I got up and walked with long strides back across the hall into the library. She was seated in a chair with her back toward me, and Free and Madeline were standing in front of her, obviously discussing something important based on their intense facial expressions.

"Excuse us for a moment," I said politely, grabbing a fistful of Marta's raven black hair and pulling her to her feet.

"Jonathan!" Madeline exclaimed.

"Not now," I growled, not bothering to look at my wife as I half dragged Marta behind me back to Royal's room.

"I can walk, dammit!" Marta protested, trying in vain to loosen my grip on her hair.

"Shut the fuck up," I said, continuing to pull her forcefully.

Once I got her into the room, I shoved her into the same seat that she'd occupied a short time ago. For a long moment, her and Royal simply stared at each other, and I was lost as to what communication was being exchanged between them. It wasn't until Royal's eyes flickered up to meet mine that I let her hair go and took a step back.

"You got a message from your lieutenant stating that there's a problem that he needs to discuss with you immediately," Royal said, passing her phone to her.

She took it without hesitation and made the call on speakerphone. My Spanish was beyond rusty, especially after being surrounded and immersed in Russian dialect for so long, but I could tell that Royal was catching every word. The call only lasted a few minutes, but it was clear by Marta's tone and body language that she wasn't the least bit happy.

"Where is she?" Royal asked once the call was disconnected.

"We don't know. All we know is that she was moved, and the trail seems to point to Georgia before going cold," Marta replied.

"Moved? By who?" I asked.

"By who owns the facility," Royal answered, still staring at Marta.

"The good news is that we found out its diplomatically owned, but the bad news is that we don't know who the diplomats are behind it,'" she said.

"I do," I said, shaking my head, growing frustrated.

"So, David has my wife *and* my daughter?" Royal asked, looking at me now.

I nodded my head, and I saw all the doubt and torment clear from his eyes.

"Then everyone that he loves will pay the price, and that means everyone connected to them. *Everyone* dies until what's mine is safely returned," Royal stated in a deadly whisper.

Chapter 10

(David)

(Four Days Later)

"How long have you been up?" Ty asked, coming out onto the back veranda and sitting at the table next to me.

My eyes didn't shift from the rising sun in the distance, but I didn't need to see her face to recognize the concern in her voice tone.

"I haven't been asleep," I replied honestly.

"David, you've barely slept in the past few days... Why don't you take something for it so that you can get some rest?"

"I'm fine," I replied.

"Bae, you're not, and I get it. I know that I'd probably be suffering from the same insomnia if I'd been the one to kill Tesha, and I can't put into words how much I love you for taking that pain for and from me. You took care of me and this family like you always do, but now I need you to take care of yourself as well."

"I'm fine, Ty," I repeated, not really wanting to have a conversation about what had happened with Tesha.

Part of me couldn't believe what I'd done, but part of me knew that I'd made the only decision that benefited my family long term. The only part that was really fucking with me was the aftermath — or more specifically the way that Stormy had cried. I knew that the loud sound of the gun going off had been what scared her and made her cry, but my conscience kept trying to convince me that she understood her mother's death. I didn't necessarily feel guilty for killing Tesha, but when I thought about how that could ultimately affect my daughter in the long term, it was impossible not to feel guilt. I was determined to die with the lie of what happened to Tesha if it ever came up for some reason, and I'd kill *anyone* who breathed a word of the truth to my daughter. Hopefully, it would never come up though because with Tesha and Tynesha being twins, Stormy wouldn't know the difference.

"I'm surprised that Carrie ain't out here with you because she's not in the bedroom," Ty said, changing the subject.

"She went into town earlier."

"Oh... have you noticed that she's been acting different lately?" she asked.

"Wouldn't you be acting different if you saw me blow a bitch's brains out while she was holding her kid?" I countered sarcastically.

"Yeah, but that's not what I meant. I felt her energy shift before that actually happened, but I can't put my finger on why I feel this way or what happened. Has she said anything to you?"

"No," I replied shortly, picking up my glass of orange juice and sipping from it.

"If she did say something to you, would you tell me?"

The tone of her question caused me to put my glass down and cut my eyes at her.

"Are you trying to start a fight?" I asked, feeling my face heat up from building anger.

"Not at all, sweetheart. I'm simply asking a straightforward question because I'm not blind to the love that you have for her. I'm not jealous of it because I know that it's not the same as you and I share, plus I agreed to making her a part of our relationship, but I'm not naïve either. I know that there are secrets between you two, but I'm telling you now that they better be harmless secrets."

"Hold up. Wait a minute. Who the fuck do you think you're talking to?" I asked, turning to face her while fighting the temptation to smack the dog shit out of her.

"Oh, I'm most definitely talking to you, my nigga. You better know that I ain't the same sweet girl from high school nor am I that bitch who needed rescuing at the gas station in Orlando. You'll *never* play in my face, and while I do fuck with Carrie in a major way, I won't hesitate to spin that bitch. Hear me?"

"Oh, I most definitely hear you, sweetheart, and now I want you to listen closely. I completely understand why you wanted your sister and your cousin dead, but if you think that I'mma just stand by and let you kill Carrie for some insignificant reason in your mind, then you got me wholeheartedly fucked up. That woman ain't did shit except help *us* from day one when you brought her into our life, and while you were off running with Roland, she was the *only* muthafucka who stood ten toes down wit me on some genuine shit. So, fuck what you talking bout because I ain't going for it. Hear *me*?!" I asked in a threatening tone.

I saw the fire flash in her hazel green eyes, but before she could say anything, the woman that had inspired this little argument stepped out onto the veranda. I'd caught sight of her out of my peripheral vision, but when I turned my attention to her, I immediately saw that something was wrong based on her tear-streaked face.

"What's wrong?" I asked, immediately getting to my feet while silently praying that it wasn't about the baby she was carrying.

"My-My family is... my family was murdered. My ex-husband, my kids, my parents... They're all gone," she sobbed, coming toward us.

I stepped away from the table and opened my arms for her to move into as my brain raced trying to understand what the fuck had just been told to me. Carrie collapsed into my arms, dissolving into tears and gut-wrenching wails of pain.

I held her tight, but over her head, I saw General Udoku come out onto the veranda, and the look on his face let me know that it wasn't good news about to leave his lips either.

"My king, I'm sorry to interrupt you right now, but there's been another... situation," he said hesitantly.

"What is it?" Ty asked.

When his eyes turned to her, they softened with sympathy, and I knew instantly that it had something to do with her.

"Our people in the States have reported multiple attacks aimed at all of you and your associates. The facility in Texas was torched, killing everyone inside. And I'm sorry to report this, my queen, but your grandmother and cousins in Georgia were killed," he replied.

"Killed? How?" Ty asked, visibly taken aback by this news.

I could sense the hesitation in Udoku to speak, but he knew that he had to spit it out.

"They were all gutted with a machete," he replied softly.

When I looked over at Ty, I could see the complete shock contort her features, and I immediately reached for her. I could tell that she was completely numb as she stepped into my arms, but I held her as close as I did Carrie. There was no way that this was a coincidence, and the brutality used was trademark cartel hits, but I wasn't beefing with the cartels. That could only mean that someone was pulling those strings, and I intended to find out who the fuck that was.

"Find out who is responsible for this. Spare no expense, take as many lives as you have to, but don't come back without answers," I demanded, locking eyes with Udoku.

He nodded once curtly before he turned around and left. I knew that there were no words that I could offer to speak to the impossible loss that either of these women were feeling, so I simply held them close to me. After a few moments, Ty pushed away from me and rushed back inside the house. I felt torn as to what I was supposed to do given the fact that Carrie was pregnant and therefore in need of more emotional support.

"You gotta keep it together for the baby, sweetheart," I whispered, kissing her on the forehead.

"I'm-I'm trying, David, but who would do this? Why kill all of these innocent people?"

"I don't know, sweetheart, but I promise you that we'll find out," I vowed.

She didn't say more. She just laid back against me, and I rested my head on top of hers... until I saw Ty pop back outside with an AK-47 in her grip. Before I had time to assess her intent, she walked over to the railing at the far end of the veranda, raised the assault rifle, and let shots ring out into the open air as she screamed like a banshee. I felt Carrie jump at the sound of the first shot, and she clung to me tightly until the only sound was the dry click of the gun's empty clip. When there were no more bullets left, it seemed like Ty's rage evaporated as she collapsed to the ground while sobbing.

"Go inside and wait for me," I whispered into Carrie's ear.

She looked up at me and nodded before giving me a quick kiss on the lips and stepping away from me. I went over to Ty, no longer feeling the anger of our heated exchanges moments ago, and picked her up off the ground. She didn't resist but instead let the gun fall to the ground as she wrapped herself around me like a frightened child. When I turned back around, I saw that the guards had rushed out onto the veranda, no doubt in response to the AK going off, but I waved them away as I carried my wife inside and up to our room. Once I put her in the bed, I sent for the doctor that we kept on the compound with us, and I instructed him to give her a sedative. When that was done, I left her in bed and went in search of Carrie. It wasn't a surprise to find her out on the upstairs balcony of our son's room, holding him tightly while silent tears continued to cascade down her beautiful face. I didn't ask her if she was okay because I knew that it was impossible for her to be after the devastating news that she'd gotten. I knew that she was probably feeling grief and guilt in equal measure due to the fact that she'd walked away from her husband and family for us. If I was being completely honest though, I knew that she'd left her old life for *me* more than anything, and it was this knowledge that had provoked me to make my position clear with Ty where Carrie was concerned. When I walked up and wrapped my arms around her and Deante, she leaned into me and sighed deeply.

"I'm so sorry, sweetheart," I said sincerely.

"It's not your fault... It's mine."

"This isn't a weight or a guilt that you get to carry all alone. The things that have happened were my calls and decisions, so I take the blame," I said, holding her tighter.

"I don't know what to do, David. I mean, how do I grieve when guilt is swallowing me?"

"I wish I knew the answer to that, bae, but I don't because I've never handled grief exceptionally well by anyone's standards. My typical move is to take my vengeance, wrap myself in it, and run through my ops like bowling pins," I replied honestly.

"Who are our ops now though? Who would do this?"

Her questions were what I'd been asking myself nonstop since the news had been spoken, and I could only think of one enemy with this much pull. The Walker family.

"My best guess is that it's the work of Royal's family because they've still been fighting to get Stormy back. Not to mention that no one else would have more of a reason to attack the facility in Texas, and two attacks so close together is anything but a coincidence," I surmised.

"But I thought that you had a foothold with at least one of the big cartels in Mexico, assuming that this was their contracted work?" she asked, looking up at me.

"That's a loyalty that's easily bought and not to be trusted, but it's okay because I've got an army at my disposal."

"If you attack with your army, it's gonna cause an international incident again like when your Uncle Umar descended on Florida," she reminded me.

"True, but that was in the United States, and we know that the Walker family doesn't operate out on the open on those shores. Russia is their home base now, especially since Royal's compound in Nigeria has been seized by me."

Her eyes went back to the beauty of the African desert as the sun continued its rise, but after a few moments, she turned all the way around to face me.

"You wanna wage a war in Russia? What's your relationship like with their dictator?" she asked.

"We don't have a relationship. Why?"

"Because what you're talking about will cause something global to happen as a repercussion. Russia is known for its long memory, so you're gonna need friends in high places if you plan to make an enemy of a country that hostile. This ain't some street shit that you're talking about anymore, David, so you gotta think bigger."

I contemplated her words and their meaning, and the truth that she spoke was real enough to make my heart beat faster. The Walkers weren't ordinary ops, which meant that however I attacked them had to be more than just coldblooded. It had to be ruthless and precise. This was about to be my true test as a king.

"So, then, the enemy of my enemy must become my friend," I said.

"And who would that be exactly?"

"Well, I know that there's enough bad blood between the U.S. and Russia to fill the entire Atlantic Ocean, but by now, I'd bet that Fathergod has made sure that they all have Russian citizenship and diplomatic immunity. Russia isn't gonna give up one of theirs to anyone... unless it's in their best interest," I replied thoughtfully.

"It sounds like you've got an idea."

"Maybe. Russia isn't a part of NATO, which means that technically, on the world stage, they don't answer to anyone. They are, however, beholden to their business partners because they can't function as a prosperous country without trade," I replied.

"Okay, I'm following your logic, but how do you plan to interrupt their trade embargo, and what does it have to do with the Walkers?" she asked, looking at me quizzically.

"If you fuck with anyone's money, I can guarantee that they won't be your friend for long. As for what that has to do with the Walkers, well if it gets out that Russia is harboring American terrorists, then that country will go to the top of everyone's shit list. My Uncle Umar had contacts within the World Court that I can reach out to and whisper into their ear. I'm sure that their memory's too long to forget the havoc the Walkers created in the States."

While I'd been explaining, she'd been nodding subtly, so I could tell that she was following my train of thought.

"Being an actual king opens doors to you that you couldn't walk through as an average street nigga, so it's important that you remember who you are. For all of our sakes," she said, looking down at our son in her arms.

I nodded in agreement, finally understanding part of what my Uncle Umar had been trying to prepare me for when it came to the heaviness of the crown I wore. I knew in my heart that he was watching over me, and I couldn't fail him.

"I'm gonna go set things in motion. Why don't you stay here with Deante and let all of his joy and innocence give you comfort?" I suggested gently.

She gave me a sad smile, but we both knew that she needed our son's love to offset the pain that was threatening to drown her. I gave both of them a quick kiss on their foreheads before turning to leave. At first, I was gonna go check on Ty, but there was no time to waste when it came to putting shit into motion, so I headed straight for my office instead. I made important yet discreet inquiries into the

Walkers' status in Russia, and I quickly found out that they'd more or less bought diplomatic immunity, and they were in favor with the president there. This wasn't news that excited me, but knowing my enemy was the only way to discover and exploit their weakness. When I learned that the world thought that Jonathan "Fathergod" Walker had died years ago when he was under lock and key in Guantanamo Bay prison, I smelled the first drip of blood in the water. Pulling on that thread led to the discovery that his wife was a former general for the U.S. military, who had coincidentally been in charge when Fathergod was at Guantanamo Bay. The bigger picture took form in my mind immediately, and in that moment, I found the first weakness to exploit. A woman was the easiest distraction for any man, especially when it was a woman that he loved. I continued digging, and when I learned that Destiny Walker had recently been killed, I understood what else had prompted the Walker family to strike with such incredible force. Before I knew it, two hours had gone by, and I finally put the phone down so that I could go check on Ty. When I didn't find her in bed, I felt unease creep up my spine, and my next move was to go find Carrie. Before I got to that wing of the house though, I ran into General Udoku in the hallway, and the look on his face spelled more bad news to be delivered.

"Now what?" I asked with rising irritation.

"It's the queen. She's left the compound, and I was just alerted that she took the jet from the airport."

I didn't ask him where she was going, but I feared the worst. I feared she was taking the fight to the enemy I'd been suspecting.

Chapter 11

(Royal)

(Two Days Later)

The tapping on the door to my bedroom distracted me from the phone in my hand, and I looked up to find Marta standing just outside my room.

"What do you want?" I asked, trying to at least be civil but hearing the ever-present anger I felt toward her.

"I was just checking on you."

"Please spare me any bullshit because I'm still working on digesting my food properly again," I replied, looking at her blankly.

"Despite what you think of me and my methods, I honestly never wanted you to be in this situation."

"What-the fuck-ever, Marta. I heard you spitting the same shit when I was unconscious, so please save me an encore performance."

The look of surprise that popped up on her face was genuine, and I immediately realized my slip of the tongue.

"So, you could hear me... which means that you heard our son's heartbeat too," she surmised, stepping tentatively into the room.

In the past couple days, we'd avoided the obvious topic of what had her stomach so huge, but that had mainly been due to my overprotective sisters hovering over me anytime Marta had been present. The only reason that she'd made it this far now was because Angel and Free were out in the streets handling business. I didn't know where my dad was, but he couldn't be far away and was undoubtedly still planning Marta's demise. He hadn't said as much, but I knew him and how he evaluated situations.

"Yeah, I heard his heartbeat... He sounds strong," I said in a softer tone.

"I'm more worried about how strong willed he's gonna be because I swear that this boy kicks the shit out of me when he wants something."

The smile on her face was something that I'd never seen before, and it gave me a window by which to observe the natural joy that motherhood brought her. Yeah, she was complaining about the baby kicking, but it was apparent that she was loving every moment of it. I better understood what I took from her once upon a time.

"I know that I've never said it... but I'm sorry about what I did to Paco. I know now that I should've made a different decision," I admitted.

The look in her eyes hardened for a second, but then she appeared to release those particular demons and gave me a slight nod. Instinctively, I knew that this was a subject that I need never broach again.

"You wanna feel him kick?" she asked, coming to stand beside me.

"I, uh, I'm not sure because..."

She ignored my uncomfortable protest by taking my free hand and slipping it under her shirt to rest on the warm flesh of her stomach. I immediately felt what could only be described as the cadence of a snare drum beating.

"What the fuck?" I said, looking up at her wide eyed.

The way that she laughed and smiled made her beautiful in a way that I'd never seen, and I realized that I was seeing the meaning behind the 'glow' that motherhood put on most women.

"I swear to you that he's been doing that ever since you started speaking a little while ago. I know that it sounds crazy, but it feels like he recognizes who you are by your voice."

"But... how?" I asked, partially awed and confused at the same time.

"I don't know how to explain it. I just know that he reacts to you. I know it's gonna sound weird, but from when I first found out that I was pregnant, I've been talking to him about you. Only the good stuff though."

"What do you mean?" I asked, looking back up at her.

"Royal, you're not an evil person. I know that you've done some fucked up shit, but underneath all of that, I believe that you still have a heart, and you possess incredible strength for someone so young in years. So, those are the things that I speak to our son about because I hope he inherits those qualities and not just our murderous instincts."

For a moment, all I could do was stare at her in bewilderment, and then, my eyes went back to her stomach where I could feel my son kicking strongly.

"What the fuck are you doing in here?" my dad asked, his voice booming loudly in the room.

I looked over to find him standing in the doorway with his gun clutched in his grip like he definitely intended to use it.

"It's okay, Pops. She was just…"

"I'm talking to her, Royal, not you. I thought that I made myself real muthafuckin clear, Marta, when I told you to stay away from my son."

I knew enough about Marta to know that she was too crazy to be afraid of my pops on an ordinary day, but she still took a step back from me, severing the physical contact that we'd been sharing.

In that moment, I realized that she wasn't afraid of my pops. She was afraid for our child. Instinct pushed me out of the bed, and before it crystalized into a clear thought, I was standing in front of Marta.

"Do I need to remind you that she's pregnant?" I asked calmly, trying to use logic to defuse the situation.

"Not my problem, and the last time I checked, a bitch being pregnant didn't affect her hearing," he replied callously.

For a moment, I simply stared at him, trying to wrap my mind around what he'd just said, and in that moment, I understood the other side of this man that my mother had known — the side incapable of forgiving.

"Not your problem? Her being pregnant with your grandson ain't your problem? Fair enough. It *is* my problem though, so let's make this the last time that you come at her like that while she's carrying my child," I said unflinchingly.

The look of surprise on his face was too genuine to be faked, and I knew that it felt completely foreign to him to be wearing it. He bounced back quick though, and suddenly, he was looking at me with the eyes of a stranger.

"Who the fuck do you think you're talking to?" he asked in a deadly whisper.

"Pops, I mean no disrespect but put yourself in my position and understand how impossible this shit is gonna be if we can't keep the peace."

"Oh, we can keep the peace just-the-fuck-fine as long as this bitch does what I tell her and you check your muthafuckin tone, patna," he replied.

"Check my tone? Ain't no tone, but I said what I said, and I need you to stop making this shit about you. It wasn't you who dropped the hammer on her son and his father; it was me. And it wasn't you who got kidnapped and tortured in Mexico; it was me. It definitely wasn't you who was in a coma for six months, so I'mma for real need you to get some perspective on shit," I said, feeling my patience wearing thin.

"I see that going through all of that made you soft," he said, shaking his head in disgust.

"What's going on in here?" Madeline asked, walking up beside my father and pulling his arm.

"What's going on is that Royal has lost his goddamn mind, talking to me like this bitch being pregnant with his kid gives her some type of breezeway pass to disobey my orders. I'm bout to learn *everybody* something real quick though," he replied, pulling the slide back on his pistol to chamber a round into the barrel.

The midnight black of his eyes radiated his lack of empathy, and for a split second, I wondered if he was intending to shoot Marta or both of us.

"I suggest you be easy... unless your memory has failed you about who I am and who I was made to be," I said in an even tone.

"Boy, bring your ass on here and tend to Truth because she's acting a whole ass about not getting the ice cream you promised her," Madeline said, pulling him out of the room before things could escalate further.

I waited until he was completely out of sight before I sat back down on my bed.

The adrenaline was racing through me, but I hadn't noticed it until this moment. I could feel Marta's gaze on me, and when I looked up at her, I immediately saw the shock that she was feeling.

"Are you okay?" I asked.

"I'm-I'm okay. It's just... I appreciate what you did," she replied genuinely.

"Stress ain't good for the baby, and the last thing that I want is for you to go into premature labor... which is why I'm gonna suggest that it might be a good idea for you to return to Mexico for now."

"I've thought about this, and honestly, it had never been my plan to stay here this long because I just wanted to negotiate the deal to align our families and then go home. You being awake changes everything though because I don't want you to miss a moment of our son's life, including his birth," she said.

"I appreciate that, but my father won't make this easy on you, and with Destiny being gone, along with my wife still missing, he's not in his right frame of mind. You're the easiest and closest target for him to take his anger out on, which means you and our baby are always in danger."

"Understood. But you will protect our child," she said confidently.

Her verbalizing those words made the truth register in my mind because I'd done just that when my father had got on the bullshit.

"You're right. I will protect our son, and right now, that means making sure that you're out of harm's way," I replied.

"I don't consider myself to be in harm's way until we know that your wife is on her way home. When we get that update, then I'll leave because I don't wanna be here to throw this in her face. Until then though, I will endure your father's antics."

I stared at her for a moment before nodding. My phone started ringing, diverting my attention as I searched for it on the bed where I'd dropped it. Once I located it and saw who was calling, I could only smile and shake my head as I answered.

"Yes, Freedom?" I asked.

I listened to her speak for a moment before looking toward my bedroom door.

"I'm fine, Free. Dad was just on one. I don't know why Madeline texted you, but you should already know that I can handle my father," I said, sitting back on the bed, facing Marta.

What Free said next took me backwards in time to the streets of London when I was much younger, less experienced, but by all accounts, more deadly.

"Don't worry, big sis. There won't be any gunplay. I won't let him provoke me, but you know that I'm not gonna let him hurt my kid. You know firsthand just how protective

I am. I want you to just stay focused out there and hit me back when you have an update," I said.

I disconnected the call after Free agreed to text me later.

"I only heard one side of that conversation, but why does it sound like your sister is more worried about you doing something to your father than the other way around?" Marta asked.

"It's a long story."

"Obviously, but it seems to be one worthy of listening to," she said, sitting in the chair next to my bed.

I hesitated, not only out of shame for some of the things that I'd done back then but also because sharing my secrets with this particular woman was something that I wouldn't have entertained six months ago. Almost dying and then being suspended in animation in a coma for half a year had changed me though. It wasn't something that I could exactly articulate, but I could feel the difference inside myself.

"My family wasn't always this close. In fact, we went to war with each other, and some would argue that I was the one to kick shit off when I took my little brother and nephew and fled the country. I still say that the war was declared when my sisters killed our mother and hid the truth from me."

"Wait, you took one of your sister's kids and your mother's son?" she asked.

"No, I took my father's newborn baby boy, and yes, I took Free's son too because I was determined to protect them from the family I didn't really know. I just thought they were killers without loyalty. Of course that didn't go over very well, as I'm sure you've heard through different sources and news reports. What wasn't made public was that during this time, I actually shot my father, Free, and I killed my sister, Destiny's first wife. So, Free knows that I ain't scared, and neither is my father, which makes for a disaster if things get too crazy. I'm guessing that Madeline knows that too because that would explain why she immediately sent Free a message about the scene that she walked in on."

Marta was doing her best to conceal her surprise, but her eyes couldn't tell that lie.

"How old were you when all of that happened?" she asked.

"I was twelve, going on thirteen years old, on the run around the globe with two kids. I'm sure that sounds unbelievable to you."

"If I hadn't done my homework on your family and learned most of this, then I'd swear that you were lying, but knowing the details makes shit make more sense," she said.

"How so?" I asked curiously.

"Well, there was some hesitation in your father when you put yourself in between us, which I thought was understandable because you're his son. But there was indecision too, and the killers that I know don't feel that. Your father knows in his heart that you won't back down, and that scares him just enough to make him think twice."

"I won't back down from anyone, especially when I'm righteous in my decision. That's how my mother raised me," I replied, feeling the pull of nostalgia on my heart.

"The other thing that made sense is why you made the decision to kill my Paco at such a young age. I'm not saying that I will ever condone what you did, or forgive it, but it does ease some of the pain to know why you felt so certain and justified in what you did. You know only too well what Paco could become capable of, even at that age, because of what had shaped your path as a killer. So, you knew that sooner than later, he'd come for revenge, meaning that he'd come for you and yours."

As much as she was speaking with certainty, I could hear the question behind her words. I nodded slowly to confirm what she was saying, feeling no pride in the cold calculation that I'd been forced to live by. A heavy silence fell between us, but it wasn't necessarily awkward. It felt like we were both mourning lost children while understanding that we both had to be better for the child getting ready to enter the world. The sudden chirp of my house's alarm system distracted both of us from the thoughts that we'd been sharing.

"What the hell is that sound?" she asked.

"An alarm that's tripped by the guards at the gate. It means that someone unexpected has arrived and is now on the grounds," I replied while getting up and lifting the edge of my bed to grab the baby Uzi that I kept there.

"Stay behind me," I said, pulling the slide to chamber the first of sixty rounds.

I led the way down the hallway and reached the alcove at the same time as Madeline and my father, both of whom had their guns up.

"Unexpected guests don't get warm welcomes, so just stay right here," I instructed Marta as I stepped out into the open with the other two guns aimed at the door.

I held up my hand to Madeline and my dad as I moved toward the door to check shit out. The security camera mounted on the wall revealed two men and two women standing on my front steps, all white people, dressed in business attire. This definitely wasn't Avon calling or a Jehovah's Witness looking to spread the good news.

"Guns down," I said, glancing over my shoulder as I motioned for Marta to come to me and take the baby Uzi.

Once she moved back out of sight, and I made sure that Madeline and my father had put their guns away, I pulled the door open.

"Can I help you?" I asked.

"Royal Walker?" one man asked.

"Depends. Who are you, and what the fuck do you want?" I replied.

"We're from Interpol," one woman said, holding out papers for me to read.

I took the papers and read what they said, but I had to read them a second time to make sure that I wasn't tripping.

"What the fuck is a Red Notice?" I asked.

"It's the equivalent of an arrest warrant used to detain an international criminal or person of interest. What is he wanted for?" Madeline asked, coming to stand beside me.

"It's not for me," I said, looking over at her, still in shock.

"Madeline Parker-Walker, by order of Interpol and the World Court, you are hereby being detained pending your extradition to the United States," one man said, producing handcuffs and taking a step toward her.

I could feel my father's presence looming menacingly, but before he could make a move, I waved him off because I'd read the fine print of the Red Notice.

"Detained on what charge?" Madeline asked.

"Treason. You conspired in the fake death and escape of Jonathan Walker while you were still a member of the United States military stationed at Guantanamo Bay. Mr. Walker is guilty of war crimes, and since you helped him escape, you're being charged with treason. Now, tell us where your husband is."

Chapter 12

(Marta)

From the shadows a few feet away, I could hear what was going on, and having been through it myself, I knew that shit was about to go bad for Madeline. Fathergod was like a lion ready to pop up out of some high grass and pounce, but he waited and continued to let the situation unfold.

"It seems like you all wasted a trip out here because I have diplomatic immunity," Madeline stated calmly.

"Correction, you *had* diplomatic immunity, but President Putin revoked that along with the diplomatic immunity of your family and all of your citizenships. I expect that your whole family will be forced to leave the country within the next forty-eight hours."

"There must be some type of mistake because we're friends of the president," Royal said.

"There's no mistake. Now, Mrs. Walker, can you step out here and place your hands behind your back? If your husband is inside, then tell him to come out."

Something about that demand kicked Fathergod into gear because, suddenly, his gun was back out, and he was moving toward the door. Within a matter of seconds, he'd pulled Royal out of the way and raised the pistol to shoulder height.

"You looking for me," Fathergod said, firing four shots in quick succession.

No screams were heard, but the sound of bodies dropping could be heard loud and clear.

"Jonathan, no," Madeline said softly.

We all knew that her plea was too little too late, but to emphasize this point, Fathergod fired four more shots into the fallen bodies and then pulled Madeline back inside before shutting the door.

"What the fuck?!" Royal exclaimed.

"Listen to me, both of you. Those people weren't door to door salesman, and there wasn't no way to negotiate our way out of being sent to our deaths. That means it was either them or us, and that was an obvious choice to be made for me. Now, we gotta get the fuck out of the country, so Madeline, you go get Truth ready while I call everybody and give them a heads up. We may be the only two wanted, but without our diplomatic immunity, I'm sure that they will be coming for everyone," Fathergod surmised.

"How are we getting out of the country?" Royal asked.

"We're gonna split up. You're gonna take all of the kids and sail out on your yacht, while Madeline and I fly out. Bone, Lil Boy, and Big Baby are already with Free and Angel, so we don't gotta worry about them," Fathergod replied decisively.

"Where do you want me to go?" Royal asked.

The fact that no one was panicked, despite Fathergod just executing what equated to four international cops, gave me a new respect for them all.

"I don't wanna know where you're headed, but we'll meet up in three days once I call you. Everyone, grab a new phone, money, and at least three of the fake passports that we keep for emergency situations," Fathergod instructed.

Both Madeline and Royal nodded before everyone started to move, but as soon as Royal turned and saw me still standing there, his whole energy shifted. I could tell by the expression on his face that in the heat of the moment, he'd completely forgotten that I was here, but he visibly adjusted quickly.

"We've gotta go," he said, coming toward me fast.

I didn't argue. I simply fell into step behind him as he headed up the hallway. We went to the library where he accessed a wall safe, and he began to pull shit out. While he did that, I sat the baby Uzi down and pulled out my phone so that I could make contact with my people and put my own plan into motion.

"Royal, if your yacht is registered to you, then it's only a certain amount of time before Interpol enlists the coast guard to board it, even if we're in international waters," I stated.

"Do you have an alternative mode of transportation readily available to get several small children out of what is sure to become a hostile environment?" he asked, not pausing in his movements.

"I do actually. I control a few of the major ports in Texas, so I can have a container ship meet us off the coast for the trip across the ocean, and then I'll have another yacht meet us before we cross into waters controlled by the U.S. After that, you can decide where we go."

He paused for a moment and turned around to face me. I could tell that he wasn't just evaluating my suggestion; he was trying to decide if he could trust me because we were talking about the lives of the little ones that he would give his life to protect. The way that his eyes traveled to my stomach, I could tell that protecting our child was on his mind too.

"Make the arrangements," he said, going back to what he needed to do right this moment.

I took to the task, and in less than ten minutes, I had all of the moving parts in motion. By that time, he had everything that he needed. Madeline met us at the door and handed Royal a sleeping toddler. After he promised to take care of her, we went outside and loaded up into the gray Range Rover. The fact that we had to step over the bloody, bullet riddled bodies of the dead Interpol officers wasn't disturbing in the least bit to me, but my eyes were on the horizon because there was no doubt in my mind that their backup was sure to be here soon. It became obvious to me that Royal was thinking along the same wavelength once we were secured behind the tinted windows of the Range Rover because he didn't drive toward the front gate. He took us around the back of his house, and we drove to the far northeast corner of his property. I didn't see a break in the fence line, but once we got closer, the chain link fence split down the middle, like it had been unzipped, and we drove straight through without issue. He stuck mainly to the back roads, and within twenty minutes, we were pulling up at the marina. We pulled straight up to the dock and hopped out. I immediately noticed that Royal made no move to hide the machine gun in his hand while he got Truth out of the SUV, and his eyes were steadily moving, which told me that he was all the way on bullshit.

This was a side of him that I never got to see for real, but the confidence that he moved with was reminiscent of the day that he'd walked into my building in Mexico City. As inappropriate as the timing was, seeing him like this was making my pussy throb with an itch that I knew he could scratch quite well. I had to physically shake the erotic images from my mind as I followed him out onto the dock and aboard the luxury yacht.

"You can either rest in the parlor or you can go pick out a room for yourself below deck before the boat is overrun with kids and nannies," he said.

"I'll get myself a room and make contact with my people so that I can get the GPS location for the rendezvous. I'll come find you when I know more."

He nodded and pointed me toward the stairs. As I made my way through the yacht and down the steps, I was admiring the beauty of the boat because it was obvious that no expense had been spared. It didn't feel like a rich man's toy though because there were pictures of Royal and his family scattered throughout the record, and I would've bet that this was a place that Royal spent a lot of time. I chose the first room that I came to at the bottom of the steps, and as soon as I saw the king-sized bed, the fatigue hit me like I hadn't slept in a lifetime. Before I could sit down and test its comfort out, my son kicked the fuck out of my bladder and forced me in the direction of the bathroom. When I was done in there, I kicked back on the bed and texted my lieutenant for an update. I was waiting on the response, but I never heard it because resting my eyes turned into being knocked the fuck out.

I awoke with a start, feeling disoriented because I didn't immediately recognize my environment until the motion of the boat registered in my mind. When I looked out of the port window, I saw that the sun had set, and the sky had morphed into a purple shade that was beautiful. I checked my phone and discovered that I'd been sleep for damn near four hours which blew my mind because I'd thought that I'd only closed my eyes for a few moments. The growling of my stomach let me know that my son knew exactly how long I'd been asleep, and he wasn't going for any type of malnourishment. The message from my lieutenant was three hours old, and it came with coordinates, so I got up out of the comfortable bed and went in search of Royal. When I opened the door, I expected to hear the sounds of children echoing throughout the yacht, but everything was eerily quiet. I went back upstairs, and I found Royal sitting in front of a wide screen TV in the parlor, watching an NBA basketball game. His eyes immediately slid in my direction, and he gave me a curious look.

"You okay?" he asked.

"Yeah, I'm fine. I was just more tired than I realized," I replied, smiling sheepishly.

"It's understandable, but I was a little worried, so I did check in on you a few times," he admitted.

"I, uh, I appreciate that..."

He nodded, but his eyes stayed on me like he was unsure if I was operating at one hundred percent. It was kinda cute to see him worried about me considering the very complicated history that we'd shared so far.

"So, where are the kids?" I asked, looking around.

"There was a change of plans before we left Russia. Madeline and my dad used their connections to make sure that all the kids were safe from deportation, as long as they agreed to leave the country. I could've stayed too, but now that we know what's going on, it's time for us to go on the offensive again. After I drop you off."

"What do you mean? What did you learn while I was sleep?" I asked, taking a seat next to him.

"The president told us that the pressure to serve up my pops and Madeline came from other countries that he's allied with, but ultimately, it was King David of Ghana who is pulling the strings. That means that he's figured out that we're the ones who went after him and his family, so the private war has officially gone public now. We're gonna take the fight to him on his turf."

I thought about what he said, trying to analyze how I could help since I was aligned with the Walkers.

"Going to Africa sounds like a suicide mission," I said, looking at him closely.

"Maybe, but we ain't never been the type to duck no smoke or run from a fight," he replied nonchalantly.

"And so where does that leave me and your son? You think that dropping us off in Mexico will somehow keep us safe? Have you forgotten that you and I are a little more connected than that?" His eyes went to the place on my chest where we had identical scars, and when his eyes came back to mine, I already knew what he was gonna say.

"The easy fix to that is to have the surgery to separate us... But that requires you to trust that I won't kill you or allow you to be killed," he said.

"Six months ago, I wouldn't have entertained the thought of giving up my life insurance policy... Shit, I wouldn't have considered it before you woke up, but since you've been awake, you've been... different."

"I feel different. I'm sure that almost dying *has* forever changed me, but honestly, it feels like you and I have reached some unspoken truce. Maybe it's the fact that you're carrying my son. I don't know; I'm just sure that I won't let anything happen to you or him. The only way to ensure that right now though is if I can do what needs to be done without worrying about my death killing both of you," he said.

I understood, but something foreign was pulling at my heart, and it was making me want to keep him on the sideline of this fight with me where it was safe. I knew that wasn't realistic though because his wife was still out there in the world, needing him to rescue her, and his loyalty wouldn't waiver on bringing her home. So, my feelings had to be put aside, and I demonstrated my ability to do that by pulling my phone out and texting my doctor to prepare for emergency surgery.

"We need to go to Colombia to have the surgery done," I said.

"That's not a problem, but it could take a few days. You don't get seasick, do you?"

"Not usually, but the morning sickness hasn't completely faded," I replied.

"Have you tried smoking weed?"

"That actually works?" I asked, surprised and skeptical.

He chuckled softly but nodded his head to let me know that it did. I was still looking at him skeptically which prompted him to reach to his left and grab half of a smoked blunt out of an ashtray.

"Let's start with this," he said, lighting it up.

The smell was potent but inviting, so I took it when he passed it my way, and I hit it cautiously. The invasion of the smoke to my lungs created an immediate desire to choke, but I held it in and let it out slowly.

"Damn," I whispered hoarsely, passing the blunt back.

His laughter was loud and genuine, and it surprised me because I'd never heard it before. We shared the rest of the blunt, and by the time it was gone, I felt like I was floating like a big ass hot air balloon.

"How do you feel?" he asked.

"Hungry as fuck."

This response caused him to laugh again as he got up off of the couch and disappeared into a different room. The sound of my phone chirping startled the shit out of me, making me laugh at myself as I pulled it out. At first, I thought that the message was from my lieutenant, and I was questioning why he sent me a video message, but once I pressed play, I saw a different face, and I was instantly sober again.

"Royal!" I called out, stopping the video, already knowing that I better wait for him.

He reappeared a few moments later with cookies and chips, but as soon as he looked at me, he set everything on the table and sat next to me.

"What's wrong?" he asked.

I held up my phone for him to see, and he went suddenly still.

"Why is David sending you messages?"

"I don't know, but it came from my lieutenant's phone," I replied.

He paused for a few seconds, and then he hit the play button.

"Hola, Marta. I figured that I would reach out and introduce myself since we haven't formally met. I'm King David. I'm the man whose son you kidnapped and held hostage while you played your twisted little games with my wife and Royal. It's funny that despite all of that, somehow you and the Walkers are as thick as thieves, but I guess that beggars can't be choosers when you're scrapping the bottom of the barrel for an alliance. Don't worry. I'm not asking you to confirm or deny anything because your trusted lieutenant had *so* much to say that I honestly got tired of hearing him talk. So, I cut his tongue out before I killed him. By the way, congrats on the baby, even though it won't replace the son that Royal took from you that night back in Florida. You got over that loss rather quickly, didn't you? You know what? That's not my business though, so let me stay on topic because there isn't much time. In every war, a person must choose a side, and I'm here to tell you that you *definitely* chose the wrong side. Like the Walkers, you're nothing more than a common criminal who has failed to see the bigger picture. Playing the game of chess isn't just about seeing the board. It's about anticipating your opponent's next move. For example, by now I'm sure that you and your comrades know that I was behind the move of Interpol issuing the Red Notice, but that was only the opening gambit. I knew that once that was set in motion that everyone's natural instinct would be to flee the country, and sure enough, your lieutenant confirmed that you and Royal are scheduled to rendezvous with a container ship. Since I've been studying Royal as my opp from the moment that he appeared in Tesha's hospital room, I know how much he loves his eighty-foot yacht, The Blue Blood. Naturally, I figured that would be his mode of transportation, but I do hope that none of the kids are on board. Except for the demon seed that you're carrying. Any who, time's up. I hope you enjoy your watery grave," David said, giving a sinister smile as he waved.

"Wh-What do you think he means?" I asked, feeling fear in the pit of my stomach.

"We've gotta get off…"

His sentence was left hanging as the rumble from the explosion could be felt beneath our feet and then came a flash of white light.

Chapter 13

(Fathergod)

"You okay, baby?"

"I'm far from okay. I don't do no running from no nigga, so this muthafucka, David, needs to die asap," I replied, careful to keep my voice down so that no one on the plane would overhear me.

"I understand, but we've gotta be smart about whatever we do because obviously he's not to be underestimated, given the power that he's wielding. Let's give it a couple of days, and then when we link up with the rest of the family, we can put together a solid plan. It'll be okay," Madeline reassured me, taking my hand in hers.

I nodded, but I couldn't deny the anxiety that I felt coursing through me because it was completely foreign to me. Being wanted by the law was nothing new, but David was a different type of opp than I usually encountered, and he was making moves that were out of the ordinary. He could never put fear in my heart; he was just making me play defense, and I didn't like that shit. I was the hunter, not the prey, and I felt the need to reassert my dominance by any means necessary.

"Did your parents get out of town?" I asked.

"Yeah, they're headed to a cabin that's off the radar, owned by friends of theirs. They'll be safe... and if anything goes wrong, they know to go get the kids."

The thought of not being there for my kids only infuriated me more, but I didn't express this to Madeline because I knew that she was dealing with her own separation anxiety by being away from our daughter. The only way that I knew how to deal was to switch to a battle-ready mind frame. We were set to land in Germany and change flights before we headed to Saudi Arabia where Madeline had a few connections that would help us with going to war with David. Once we had a working plan, I'd send for Free, Angel, Bone, Lil Boy, and Big Baby. If I knew Royal, he'd already have his boots on the ground in Africa by then because he'd made quite a few connections over there years ago. He didn't have the power of a king, but he knew enough hired guns to knock a nigga's crown off. Being that this was most definitely personal to Royal, I knew that he wasn't gonna spare anyone, but I had to make sure that he stayed clear headed because the goal was to win this war without losing another person that I cared about. Destiny's death still hurt, and I was using that pain to feed the rage deep within me.

"Babe?"

"Huh?" I replied, looking over at Madeline.

"You're squeezing my hand," she replied, smiling.

I loosened my grip while shaking my head in an attempt to regain control of my emotions.

"I'm sorry, sweetheart."

"It's okay. I understand how much stress is on your shoulders, but remember that I'm here," she said.

"I know you are, and I love you for that. I don't need you on the front line with me though, so I hope you're not gonna fight me on this."

"Fight you? No. I'm just gonna remind you that I'm military trained and more lethal than any woman you've ever met," she replied, smiling sweetly.

I knew that I couldn't argue with her credentials, so I wasn't about to try. When the time came, I would find some way to keep her safe, even if I had to knock her little ass out.

"Can you turn that up?" a woman asked.

When I looked to my left, I saw a cute blonde female talking to a passing steward, and she was pointing toward the TV projection screen a few feet away. My curiosity caused me to actually read the breaking news report, and what I saw made my heart seize in my chest.

"Babe, what's wrong?" Madeline asked.

"Royal," I whispered, feeling sick to my stomach.

I heard her gasp in shock, and I knew immediately that she was reading about the luxury yacht that had exploded into pieces just outside of Russia, which technically put it in international waters. In my heart, I wanted to deny the truth, but the fact that they had the name of Royal's yacht plastered across the screen made denial impossible. They hadn't officially identified anyone aboard the vessel, but it did say that the remains of five to six people were found, and in my mind, that accounted for Royal, Marta, and the crew. The only person that I gave a fuck about was my son though.

"He can't-He can't be gone," I whispered, shaking my head as my tears fell.

Madeline took my hand in hers, but I could barely feel her touch because I was completely numb from the inside out. Mentally, I was trying to make sense of it, and I couldn't. How could I have lost two of my children in such a short amount of time? In some ways, it hurt more to lose Royal because I'd had such little time with him due to the fact that I'd missed the first eleven years of his life. It was too hard to believe that his young life had been extinguished already, especially since he'd beat the odds after coming back to us from being in a coma. The news report was claiming that it had been some type of gas leak that resulted in an explosion, but I could feel the bullshit in my bones about that explanation. This was David's doing or someone that he'd hired in Russia.

"How long before our flight touches down?" I asked, wiping the tears from my face.

"About an hour," Madeline replied.

I nodded silently and began to plot my next move. With Marta gone that meant that the support of the cartels was lost, and with Madeline being wanted by the U.S. government, there was no way that any of her military contacts were good right now. We were out in the cold, but definitely still a formidable enemy, and David was about to know that. I pulled my phone out and sent a group text to Free and Angel, knowing that this news would devastate them but needing to tell them before they happened to see a news report wherever they were. Once that was done, I tried to figure out how best to launch an attack against David, but I wasn't finding one fucking weakness to exploit. The nigga had me and my family scattered in the wind, running for our lives without any real allies to depend on. This was a position that I'd never found myself in, not even when I'd been in a prison cell.

The only thing that we still had was money, and that was a power within itself. For the remainder of our flight, I used my phone to access and move large amounts of money from different offshore accounts until I'd liquidated fifty million in U.S. currency. Once that was done, I tasked Free with getting it to the right African mercenaries with instructions to deliver King David's head asap. When we landed in Germany to switch flights, I couldn't shake the feeling that I was running away from a fight like some part of me was bitch, and that was something that I just couldn't do.

"I'm not going with you to Saudi Arabia," I said, stopping Madeline in the middle of the airport terminal.

"What do you mean? What are you talking about, Jonathan?"

"I can't run from this nigga, sweetheart. He's responsible for two of my kids being dead, and he has the luxury of pushing buttons from the safety of his mansion. I can't let that shit slide," I said, shaking my head.

"Baby, I get it, and I feel your pain, but we still gotta be smart about this. You just put a huge bounty on his head, so why not give that a chance to work first?"

"Because paying someone to knock a nigga off is business, and this shit right here is *personal*! I wanna be the one to make him bleed until his last drop is drained," I stated passionately.

"Okay, Jonathan, just stop and think for a moment. You already know that he's hiding behind his official title as king, and that carried enough juice to get us deported from a country that was making millions of dollars harboring us. Do you honestly believe that he'd be stupid or careless enough to allow any of us to enter Africa? I'd bet that we're wanted criminals there too, as well as anywhere else that he's made an alliance with since he officially took power. You're smart enough to know that you don't assassinate a dictator or a president on some up close and personal shit. You do it from a distance. At the very least, you throw a rock and hide your hand," she explained patiently.

I heard the truth in her words, but I for real wasn't trying to hear that shit. I just wanted to kill this nigga and be done with it because I knew with absolute certainty that *any* nigga could be got.

"You've asked me to trust you, and now I'm asking you to do the same," she said, extending her hand toward me.

The love in her eyes was like balm on the wounds of my heart, and it forced me to take her hand in my own. We walked to our terminal and quickly boarded our flight to Saudi Arabia where the prince had told us that we were welcome to stay in the royal palace for as long as we desired.

"Can you bring me a double shot of tequila, no ice?" I requested to a passing stewardess.

"No problem, sir. I'll be back momentarily."

"Getting drunk isn't a good idea," Madeline warned.

"I'm not getting drunk. I'm just taking the edge off."

I could feel her desire to argue, but she bit a hole in her tongue just to keep her mouth shut. A few moments later, my drink arrived, and I took a healthy swig as I got comfortable in my seat. Madeline took my hand in hers and gave it a gentle squeeze, causing me to look over at her. She gave me a sad smile that conveyed her love and sympathy before she leaned over and kissed me softly. When she pulled back, she looked at me quizzically before taking the drink from my hand and sniffing it.

"What are you doing, bae?" I asked, thinking that she was trippin.

"Your breath tasted funny when I just kissed you, and your drink smells weird."

"Weird? Maybe it's just been a while since you smelled tequila considering that we drink mostly vodka these days," I said, taking my drink back from her.

"No, I'm serious, Jonathan. I can't exactly say what it is that I'm tasting, but it leaves a vanilla aftertaste, and tequila don't do that."

I was getting ready to protest further when I was hit by a sudden wave like I'd actually drank a whole bottle of tequila. I had to shake my head to clear my thoughts. My vision swam, and my stomach felt queasy, which was enough to make me rethink my conclusion that Madeline was trippin. I immediately began to look around for the female stewardess who'd served me my drink, but no one that I saw moving up and down the aisles looked familiar to me. I did catch sight of two men, one white and the other one Black, that I'd never seen before, but they caused a familiar tingling to rise up in my chest. "Air Marshals," I whispered out of the side of my mouth. I felt her tense up beside me, but I remained calm and relaxed, bringing the glass back to my lips as if I intended to drain its contents. I didn't make contact with either of the air marshals, but I could feel them closing in on our position. That meant that I needed to make something happen fast.

"Excuse me, sir, can you freshen up my drink?" I asked a passing steward.

Even in my slightly disoriented state, I could spot the nervousness in his demeanor, and that was all the confirmation that I needed about there being some type of play in motion.

"Uh, s-sure, sir. I can get that for you," he replied, extending his hand.

I moved as if I intended to hand my drink to him, but instead, I threw it in his face as I hopped up out of my seat and grabbed him by his throat. My grip was crushing on his windpipe, but I could care less because I was using him as a moving shield by pushing him backwards into the approaching air marshal. I could tell that I'd caught the cop off guard too because his reaction was super slow, and by the time he was reaching for his gun, I was only a few feet away. With a vicious twist, I snapped the steward's neck and shoved him into the marshal with my left hand while I threw a right hook at him that laid him out flat. I quickly scrambled over him to grab the Springfield .45 he'd dropped, hearing the commotion of the other air marshal behind me somewhere. Once the gun was in my grasp, I spun back around, intending to fire, but I found my wife in my sights because the marshal had his gun to her head while using her body to shield him.

"Drop it, Walker, or…"

He never got to finish his threat before I double tapped the trigger and added two holes to his face for him to breathe out of. Passengers screamed in fear and hysteria, but Madeline was completely calm as she picked up the dead marshal's gun and came toward me.

"What's our move?" she asked.

I looked toward the door of the plane and saw that it had already been closed, which only left one option in my mind.

"We get this bird in the air," I said, motioning for her to follow me.

I had no idea if there were more air marshals onboard, so I kept my eyes wide open, despite me feeling more sluggish as the drugs in my drink continued to work their way through my system. When we made it to the front of the plane, I spotted the stewardess who'd laced my tequila, and when our eyes locked, her guilt was apparent. I put a bullet in her leg without hesitation and then grabbed her by her hair before she crumbled to the floor.

"I'm only gonna ask you one time. What's the play, and who's involved?" I demanded.

"I don't-I don't know. I was just told to serve you the drink," she sobbed.

"Your mistake," I said, putting the pistol to her head and blowing her brains all over the seats and passengers behind her.

More screams ensued, but my focus was on the cockpit door. I didn't waste time knocking. I just upped the pistol and fired six shots where I estimated the co-pilot was sitting. I shot the lock off of the door next, and within seconds, Madeline and I were inside.

"Put the radio down and taxi for takeoff," I instructed calmly.

"We're-We're not cleared," the pilot replied.

I looked at the barely breathing, shot, and bleeding copilot, and then I shot him twice in the head.

"Are you sure that's your answer?" Madeline asked the pilot.

No more excuses came from his mouth, and within moments, we were moving. Immediate radio chatter started as people told him to stop, no, and don't because it was clear that he was preparing to take the big 747 airborne. He didn't even bother to do a preflight check. He just turned up the first runway that he came to and pushed the throttle all the way up. Within a few moments, we were wheels up, heading for the clouds, but I didn't feel any safer than when we'd been on the ground. I waited patiently for the plane to level off, and then, I got back on my bullshit.

"Engage the autopilot," I demanded.

Once he complied, I spun him around in the chair and put the warm barrel of the pistol to his forehead.

"I would suggest that you start talking," Madeline said.

"All-All I know is that I was told not to takeoff until you two were apprehended and escorted off of the plane. I don't even know why they wanted you," he insisted.

"Who is *they*?" I asked.

"The word that we got was the American CIA, MI6, and Interpol gave the collective order."

I didn't know if the surprise that I felt was obvious, but I knew that when I looked at Madeline, I could see the emotions on her face. In all honesty, we shouldn't have been surprised though because the charge of treason definitely hit differently than any other crime that I'd been attached to. It didn't matter how they knew how to find us; the real question was where in the world did we go to hide at this point?

"How much fuel do you have?" I asked.

"We-We just refueled."

"Where are we going, bae?" she asked.

I honestly had no clue, and that scared me more than a little bit. A crazy and rogue thought popped into my head, causing me to back away from the pilot and look around the cockpit. It took me a few moments, but I found what I was searching for in a cabinet, and I let my crazy idea continue to grow.

"Jonathan, where are we going?" she asked again.

When I looked back at her, I knew that she wasn't gonna like the answer, but the truth was better than a lie.

"We're gonna die, sweetheart. That's our best move."

Chapter 14

(David)

"You look like you're deep in thought."

I looked up to find Carrie standing in the doorway of my office, but it took me a minute to fully pull myself back into the present and see her.

"Yeah, I guess you could say that," I replied, sighing tiredly.

She came in and sat on the corner of my desk, giving me a concerned look.

"You've been in here for hours, David. I think it's time that you rest a little. Tynesha will come back home when she's ready."

"I know that, and that's not really what I'm worried about," I said.

"What is it then?"

When I looked in her eyes, I saw the sincerity behind her desire to help me, and it reassured me that she wouldn't judge me for my latest moves.

"I had a bomb put onboard of Royal's yacht because I figured that he'd flee the country in that, and my assumption was confirmed when Marta's second in command was kidnapped and delivered to me. According to the news reports, the yacht exploded about an hour ago just outside of Russia, killing everyone onboard," I said.

"Okay... are you having second thoughts about your decision?" she asked, moving from the desk and sitting in my lap by straddling me.

"No, not at all. I was just sitting here trying to figure out what my next move needs to be. I'd thought that Ty was headed for Russia, but I was wrong because the plane never made it farther than Nigeria."

"Nigeria? I don't know what she could be doing there besides recruiting mercenaries for whatever move she has planned in her mind," she replied.

"We've gotta move as one though and never off of emotions."

"I agree, bae, and you know that eventually, Ty will come to her senses. For now, I think you just need to focus on what's in front of you," she said, putting her arms around my neck and kissing me with a swiftly building passion.

Sex had been the farthest thing from my mind when she'd come into the room, but her mouth had a way of hypnotizing and possessing me so that all I wanted was her. My hands found their way under her white silk shirt where I unhooked her bra, freeing her succulent, firm titties for me to fondle tenderly. I could feel her breathing change as my thumbs grazed and caressed her nipples.

"We should take this to the bedroom," I suggested, breathing heavily in anticipation.

"We could... but there's no time like the present," she whispered, reaching down in between us and pulling my hard dick free of my boxers and slacks.

There was no protest coming from me as she slid her booty shorts to the side while guiding my dick inside of her hot pussy. My hands came from under her shirt and immediately went to her thick ass cheeks where I grabbed onto her possessively and pulled her downwards until every inch of me was buried inside her. She grabbed ahold of my face and kissed me from the depths of her soul while setting a steady rhythm that allowed her to rise and fall like a fast heartbeat. Her pussy was squeezing my dick like it was desperate to choke the cum out of it, but I fought the urge to seek complete satisfaction quickly. Instead, I was living in the enjoyment of how wet and tight she was. On average, she had some good pussy, but her being pregnant elevated her shit to a new level that I got to explore as she stretched and molded us together like moist clay. The fact that she was in control was hella sexy until my need became too insistent to ignore, and I was forced to stand up with her so that I could sit her on my desk. Without losing rhythm, she wrapped her legs around my back, allowing me to dive even deeper inside of her sacred temple.

"David," she moaned, clutching me tightly.

Her pussy was so wet that it was sounding off like an Olympic high diver hitting the water with a perfect score. I was so ready to cum that I could hear my knees rattling like two dice being shook, and there was absolutely nothing preventing my next roll.

"So, this is what you two do when I'm not around?"

The sound of Ty's voice made my eyes pop open as I looked around Carrie's head, and the sight of her standing in the doorway froze me in mid stroke like I'd done something wrong.

"Ty-Tynesha, when did you get back?" I stammered, trying to catch my breath.

"Just now. Please don't stop on my account though."

"Are you gonna watch?" Carrie asked, looking back at her.

"It wouldn't be the first time, but no, I'm gonna wait for you two in the downstairs living room," Ty replied before walking away.

There was a certain twinkle in her eyes that caused an alarm to go off in my head, but the moment that Carrie started moving again, I lost my train of thought.

"Wait," I said weakly.

"Uh un, just fuck me one last time," she demanded, using her hips and legs to pull me back inside her.

My body reacted on its own, and the next thing that I knew, I was back to pounding her pussy like a boxer working a speed bag. Within a few moments, we came together nosily, but I didn't get to bask in the afterglow because my mind immediately went back to Ty. I pulled my dick out of Carrie and fixed my clothing, even though my mind was analyzing Ty's energy from a few moments ago.

"Listen, something doesn't feel right, so I don't want you to go down here with me," I said.

"What are you talking about? Why are you acting like you and I fucking is some type of secret that was just exposed?"

"It's not that. It's just... I don't know, but I can tell that Ty is up to something, and I'd feel better figuring out what that is without you there. I don't want her directing any bullshit at you," I explained.

She stared at me for a few seconds, and then, she slid down off the desk, opened the top drawer, and pulled out one of my pistols.

"What are you doing?" I asked.

"Taking precautions, now come on," she said, giving me a quick kiss as she tucked the pistol into the back of her shorts and pulled her shirt down over it.

I was still wanting to discuss this, but Carrie was already headed out of the room, leaving me no option except to follow her.

We found Ty sitting on the couch, scrolling through her phone, which wasn't surprising. The surprising part was the fact that General Udoku and a handful of soldiers were posted up against a wall not far from her.

"What's going on, Ty?" I asked.

"Nothing much, just admiring your handiwork. I'm assuming that you were the cause of the explosion on Royal's yacht, right?" she asked.

"It was a necessary move," I replied somewhat defensively.

"Absolutely, and I'm not questioning what you did in the slightest. I do have a different question for you though, husband. Do you remember which one of us is the queen and which one is the concubine?"

"Huh?" I replied.

"Ty, what are you doing?" Carrie asked.

"I'm just talking to the king and trying to get some understanding. What are you doing, Carrie... besides trying to take my spot?" Ty asked, looking up from her phone with a piercing stare aimed at Carrie.

"You're fucking trippin," Carrie said defensively.

I could feel the tension rising along with the temperature, which caused me to step in front of Carrie in case shit went sideways.

"General Udoku, I want you and your men to wait outside while we handle this family matter privately," I instructed.

At first, I was unsure if he'd heard me because no one moved, but something about the sudden smile that appeared on Ty's face told me that there was something else going on that I wasn't aware of.

"It's okay, Udoku. I'll be out to join you momentarily," Ty said.

"Very well, my queen," Udoku replied, signaling for his men to follow him.

For a moment, my mind was scrambled because there was no way in hell that Ty's word was carrying more weight than mine.

"Who the fuck do you think you are?" I asked, fighting to control my anger.

"I know exactly who I am, sweetheart, Queen Tynesha Bishop. The question is who the fuck is the woman you're standing in front of with your predictable ass?"

"Look, I don't know what type of game you're playing, but no one has time for the bullshit. We need to focus on our next move," I said.

"Our next move? Forgive me, husband, but it didn't seem like you were worried about any moves besides sticking your dick inside of Carrie before I walked in on you. Have your thoughts returned to the more pressing issues now that you got your nut?"

The sound of Carrie giggling behind me almost made me smack the dog shit out of her, but I kept my focus on Ty because I now understood that she was leading up to something.

"You talking like you got a sudden issue with me fucking Carrie. Where's this new jealousy coming from?" I asked.

"Jealousy? I don't think a woman can be jealous when it's her nigga's dick that's being given away. I believe territorial is the better terminology, and to answer your question, you know that I've *always* been territorial. I just learned how to bite my tongue until the confrontation became necessary," Ty replied.

"And you feel like now is the time for a confrontation about who I'm fucking when there's other more important shit going on?"

"Well, it's a little deeper than that, David. I'd say that now is the time to make my power play and secure the future that I can live with. I mean, think about it. The cartels are sure to be in disarray, thanks to you getting rid of Royal *and* Marta in that two for one fire sale. The rest of your very powerful enemies are running for their lives, literally, and I've very quietly consolidated power between those who were loyal to Royal in Nigeria and those loyal to me here in Ghana. The only thing that was left was to remove the king from the throne, and given your unfortunate history when it comes to lover's quarrels, I doubt that too many questions will be asked," Ty explained.

"Ah, so your play is to somehow get rid of me and Carrie so that you can have it all?" I asked, nodding in understanding.

"Who said anything about getting rid of Carrie?" Ty asked, smiling devilishly.

I opened my mouth to speak, but before a syllable could pass my lips, I felt the barrel of a pistol shoved up against the base of my skull.

"C-Carrie, what are you doing?" I asked, unable to hide my shock.

"Well, I believe that it was you who said that in every war, you must pick a side. Ty and I talked it over, and we chose to side with each other because that's the only way to avoid us falling out over your dick."

"It's good dick though," Ty said, chuckling.

"You can't be serious," I said.

"Oh, no, we're dead ass serious, boo. I mean, why should we let you keep fucking us until we're so blinded that we fuck each other over just to have you? Shaomi did that, and we see how that turned out," Ty said, still smiling.

"I see... So, Carrie, how do you know that Ty won't do you just like she did Shaomi?" I asked.

"She won't," Carrie insisted.

"Why would I? Carrie is my partner in all of this. Two queens and no king sounds like the modern era finally came home to the African continent."

"Oh, you're partners? Well then, surely your partner told you that she's pregnant again with my child," I said, smiling.

The falter of Ty's smile immediately told me that she'd just been hit with a surprise, and it wasn't a pleasant one.

"Muthafucka," Carrie mumbled under her breath while shoving the gun harder into the back of my head.

"Pregnant, you say? Well, she didn't share the good news with me, but I figured that she was keeping a secret or two. It don't matter though," Ty insisted.

"It doesn't? You sure? Because even when I'm dead and gone, you'll be forced to see our beautiful baby grow up, knowing all the while that Carrie was the last one to be blessed with a love child from me."

"David, shut the fuck up!" Carrie growled, smacking me over the head with the pistol.

The blow forced me to my knees, but I knew that silence wasn't an option at this point.

"I bet that you can still smell the sex on her right now," I said, locking eyes with Ty.

I could see the hatred and anger entwined with the hazel green swirl that was spinning faster around her iris, so I knew that I was getting to her.

"Don't listen to him, Ty. He's just trying to fuck up our plan," Carrie insisted.

"Am I lying though? Are you pregnant or nah?" I asked while still staring at Ty.

Her eyes shifted away from mine and up toward Carrie, who was still standing behind me.

"It don't matter if I'm pregnant or not. All that matters is that you no longer dictate our future."

Carrie might not have noticed Ty's sudden silence, but I was hearing it loud and clear, and I knew what it was gonna lead to.

"What's wrong, Ty? Are you scared to ask the question that's burning the front of your brain?" I asked.

"And what question would that be, David?" Ty retorted.

"I'm sure that you wanna know whose pussy is better, seeing as how I've fucked so many different women in your circle. Maybe you wanna know whose pussy was the best between you, Tesha, Shaomi, your mom, and Carrie," I taunted.

The tightness of her jaw told me that if this hadn't been a thought or question rolling around her mind before, it damn sure was one now.

"Ty, don't feed into this," Carrie pleaded, sounding a lot like she was afraid suddenly.

Ty didn't respond, but the way that she was staring at me told me that she most definitely wanted to hear this. I put an expression on my face like I was really going into deep thought to figure out what my response would be, but I already knew what I was gonna say.

"If you really want the truth, sweetheart, I'll tell you... I swear to you on the lives of *all* my children that... Carrie has the best pussy, mouth, and ass I've ever had in my life," I stated proudly.

"Shoot him," Ty replied with hatred coating her words.

I laughed right to her face, even as I heard Carrie behind me pulling the slide on the pistol. I kept right on laughing as she put the gun to the back of my head, and the expression on Ty's face just kept getting funnier. Until Carrie pulled the trigger.

Chapter 15

(Ty)

When David's body dropped, so did my heart, but I kept a neutral expression on my face. So many emotions surged through me, and not the ones that I'd expected to feel when I'd first hatched this diabolical plan. I couldn't deny that I had love for David, but I'd stopped being in love with him a long time ago. I'd tried my best to love him, but despite my best efforts, I'd had no idea how to reclaim those feelings from before. So, I'd simply been existing, waiting for the moment when the picture-perfect world would come crashing down. Now that it had actually happened though, I was experiencing a feeling that I hadn't expected. Regret. Looking at Carrie, I could tell that she was trying to hold it together, but her deep breaths quickly turned into her hyperventilating, and before I knew it, she was on her knees, sobbing hysterically. Her pain was palpable, and I could tell by just watching her that she was forever broken by what she'd done. I had to admit that it took a certain type of ruthlessness to fuck a nigga and then blow his brains out, especially when you so obviously loved him. The way that her cries quickly rose to wails of pain let me know that full blown, snot-crying hysteria was just around the next corner, and nobody had time for that shit.

"Bitch, shut the fuck up before you cause one of the kids to come down here," I said while texting Udoku to come back inside.

I could tell that it was a struggle, but she managed to pull her shit together enough to at least put her hands over her mouth to muffle her cries. Within a few moments, General Udoku reappeared at my side, awaiting instruction.

"Take his body outside, decapitate him, and send me a picture of his head so that I can collect the fifty-million-dollar bounty," I said.

"Right away, my queen."

He snapped his fingers, and two soldiers appeared to remove David's body. For a minute, I thought that Carrie was gonna try to fight them, but she let it happen, and a few seconds later. it was just the two of us alone in the room.

"Look at the bright side. You just became a multimillionaire," I said.

She looked up at me, and for a split second, the mask that she habitually wore slipped enough for me to see how she really felt about me.

"At what cost? Do you honestly believe that all the money in the world will replace what David meant to his kids or to what he could've contributed to their lives?"

"Don't you think that those are questions you should've asked or contemplated *before* you splattered his shit? More importantly though, have you forgotten the major fact that we just took the target off of *all* of our kids' backs?" I asked.

She didn't verbally respond, but the way that she clamped her mouth shut told me that she understood the truth that I'd just spoken. When my phone vibrated in my hand, I hesitated to look at it because I knew what I'd find in my messages, but I had no choice except to finish what I started. I spared the picture a brief glance before I forwarded it to Freedom Walker along with my bank account information. Within ten minutes, I received a conformation email from my Swiss banker letting me know that a fifty-million-dollar deposit had been made and asking how I wanted it distributed. I gave General Udoku the ten million I'd promised him with instructions for him to compensate all of our troops from here to Nigeria. I dropped ten million in Carrie's account, and then I hid my thirty million for the inevitable rainy day. I couldn't say that I felt good about the moves that I'd made, but deep down, I knew that I'd done what was necessary to end the cycle of violence that David had locked us in for years. As I looked with disgust at the still blubbering woman on her knees, I seriously contemplated shooting her soft ass, but her having to live with what she did was a much better fate.

"You've got your money so get your son and get the fuck out of my house," I said, not bothering to hide my loathing.

"Wh-What? Why would I leave?"

"Because you're not welcome here. I mean, you *did* just murder my husband, so what type of bitch would I be to let you and your little bastards live under my roof?" I asked logically.

"Tynesha, I did that for *you*! I did it for *us*! How are you gonna turn your back on me and my kids when you know that the only family that we have left is in this house with you and the rest of David's kids?"

"Bitch, the only family that you have left just got carried out and dismembered. Unless you wanna end up like him, I'd suggest that you just take your money and leave," I warned savagely.

For an instant, her tears stopped, and the bright light of realization dawned clearly in her brown eyes. There was never room for two queens on the chess board that I was using, and now she understood that she'd always been the pawn masquerading as something more valuable. The reality was that she was expendable and nothing more. She didn't voice her understanding, but she did pick herself up off of the floor, still clutching the gun in her hand. I knew that every fiber in her body wanted to shoot me, but she was smart enough to know that my army would cut her and her son down within seconds. As she turned to leave, I thought that I detected the ghost of a smile on her face, but the shadows in the room made me doubt myself. I waited in the living room, and five minutes later, she came walking back through, carrying her sleeping son.

"Thanks for everything, Ty... I'll never forget it," she said, lying the gun down on the table in front of me.

I didn't respond, and I didn't get up to see her out. I got comfortable on my throne because I planned to be here for a long time.

Chapter 16

(Free)

(Two Days Later)

"Ma'am, we're getting reports of a storm coming in from the direction that we're headed. If we continue on this course, then we'll run straight into it," the captain said.

I raised my binoculars to the clouds, looking off into the distance at the swirling dark purple clouds moving with dangerous intent. From what I could tell, the weatherman was about one hundred percent accurate, but that didn't mean shit to me.

"If you wanna beat the storm, then I suggest that you drive the boat faster, but under no circumstances do we turn back before we reach the island in the distance," I said, looking pointedly at the captain.

"Yes, ma'am," he replied, backing away.

"Free, are you sure about this?" Bone asked from beside me.

"I know my dad, bae, and he wouldn't just accept the fact that a plane was gonna crash with him and Madeline on it."

"Yeah, but that plane hit a mountain one hundred miles from here, killing everyone onboard, and we've searched at least six islands in the last couple days," he replied gently.

"You're right, and we have. But this stretch of ocean is the only body of water between the airport where they took off and the mountain that the plane crashed into. So, if they were gonna bail out, then somewhere around here is where it had to happen," I reasoned, looking over at him.

I saw the love and support in his eyes, and I needed both of those things more than doubt right now. Bone must've sensed that too because he pulled me into his arms and kissed the top of my head.

"I'm with you, bae. I know just how tough your dad is, plus there's no way that he would die before you get to tell him that you won the war, and you got David's head to prove it."

I took half a step back and looked up at him with an expression of confusion.

"What do you mean that I won the war? The war ain't over yet," I stated.

"But I thought... well, because David is dead, so I figured..."

"David being dead is great, but that don't square the bill. I only want his wife to think that it does, which was why I actually paid her the money," I said.

"Okay... so, what's your next move?"

"David's entire bloodline must suffer before it's completely finished and they're annihilated. All of that will take time though. This is a war that won't end with our generation, and it's a beef that our kids have inherited," I replied.

He couldn't hide the shock in his eyes, and I knew that it was because we'd always talked about keeping our kids away from all of the bullshit the streets had to offer. The harsh reality was that the sins of the parents befell the children, no matter what, but unlike most parents, I intended to shield my children by allowing them to embrace the truth. Lies would only make them vulnerable and weak, and that wasn't the cloth that a Walker was cut from.

"Free! Free, look!"

The excitement in Angel's voice caused me to look across the deck at her, and then, I raised my binoculars in the direction that she was pointing. At first, I didn't see what the fuck had her so giddy, but then, I noticed smoke billowing toward the sky coming from the island that we were headed toward.

"What is it?" Bone asked.

It felt like my heart was in my throat, but after a few seconds, I found the words to speak.

"It's him... It's my Fathergod..."

THE END... FOR NOW.

Lock Down Publications and Ca$h Presents
Assisted Publishing Packages

Due to an increase in the price of services we have increased our prices. The prices below reflect the price increase as of 11/1/24.

BASIC PACKAGE	UPGRADED PACKAGE
$699	**$1000**
Editing	Typing
Cover Design	Editing
Formatting	Cover Design
	Formatting
	Upload eBooks to Amazon
	Upload Paperback to Amazon
ADVANCE PACKAGE	**LDP SUPREME PACKAGE**
$1,400	**$1,700**
Typing	Typing
Editing (line editing/content)	Editing (line editing/content)
Cover Design	Cover Design
Formatting	Formatting
Copyright Registration	Copyright Registration
Proofreading	Proofreading
Upload eBooks to Amazon	Set up Amazon Account
Upload Paperback to Amazon	Upload eBooks to Amazon
	Upload Paperback to Amazon
	Advertise on LDP's Amazon and Facebook Page

***

Other services available upon request.
Additional charges may apply

Lock Down Publications
P.O. Box 944
Stockbridge, GA 30281-9998
Phone: 470 303-9761
Email: lockdownpublications@gmail.com

Submission Guideline

Submit the first three chapters of your completed manuscript to ldpsubmissions@gmail.com. In the subject line add **Your Book's Title**. The manuscript must be in a Word Doc file and sent as an attachment. Document should be in Times New Roman, double spaced, and in size 12 font. Also, provide your synopsis and full contact information. If sending multiple submissions, they must each be in a separate email.

Have a story but no way to send it electronically? You can still submit to LDP/Ca$h Presents. Send in the first three chapters, written or typed, of your completed manuscript to:

LDP: Submissions Dept
P.O. Box 944
Stockbridge, GA 30281-9998

DO NOT send original manuscript. Must be a duplicate. Provide your synopsis and a cover letter containing your full contact information.

Thanks for considering LDP and Ca$h Presents.

NEW RELEASES

BLOODLINE OF A SAVAGE 1-3
THESE VICIOUS STREETS 1-3
RELENTLESS GOON 1-3
BY PRINCE A. TAUHID

THE BUTTERFLY MAFIA 1-3
BY FUMIYA PAYNE

A THUG'S STREET PRINCESS 1&2
BY MEESHA

CITY OF SMOKE 3
BY MOLOTTI

GET IT IN SLUGS 1 &2
BY B. STALL

STANDING ON HER BUSINESS 1&2
BY DG SANTANA

STEPPERS 1,2&3
THE REAL BADDIES OF CHI-RAQ
BY KING RIO

THE LANE 1&2
BY KEN-KEN SPENCE

THUG OF SPADES 1&2
LOVE IN THE TRENCHES 2
CORNER BOYS
BY COREY ROBINSON

TIL DEATH 3
BY ARYANNA

THE BIRTH OF A GANGSTER 4
BY DELMONT PLAYER

PRODUCT OF THE STREETS 1-3
BY DEMOND "MONEY" ANDERSON

NO TIME FOR ERROR
BY KEESE

MONEY HUNGRY DEMONS 1-2
BY TRANAY ADAMS

HUB CITY MENACE 1-3
BY J. WHITE

A THUGGISH PASSION 1&2
LAND OF DA HOOLIGANZ 1-4
KILLAZ ON STANDBY 1&2
BY IRA B.

FO'EVA ROLLIN 1&2
BY ASSA RAYMOND BAKER

THE LEVEL UP 1&3
BY LUXURY KING

Coming Soon from Lock Down Publications/Ca$h Presents

IF YOU CROSS ME ONCE 6
ANGEL V
By Anthony Fields

A THUGS STREET PRINCESS 3
By Meesha

CORNER BOYS 2
By Corey Robinson

THA TAKEOVER
By Keith Chandler

BETRAYAL OF A G 2
By Ray Vinci

SAVAGE FAMILY EMPIRE 1&2
SOULLESS GOON 1,2&3
THE DIRTY SIDE OF MONEY 1,2&3
By Prince

FOR MY ENEMY'S SAKE
AMBITIONS OF A SLIDER
FRESH OFF DA PORCH
By IRA B.

THE TRUCKLOAD 1-4
TIPPIN' THE SCALES 1-3
BAD BITCHES WIT GUNZ 3
PROBLEM SOLVED 2
By Christopher "Diesel" Hornezes

Available Now

RESTRAINING ORDER 1 & 2
By **CA$H & Coffee**

LOVE KNOWS NO BOUNDARIES 1-3
By **Coffee**

RAISED AS A GOON I, II, III & IV
BRED BY THE SLUMS I, II, III
BLAST FOR ME I & II
ROTTEN TO THE CORE I II III
A BRONX TALE I, II, III
DUFFLE BAG CARTEL I II III IV V VI
HEARTLESS GOON I II III IV V
A SAVAGE DOPEBOY I II
DRUG LORDS I II III
CUTTHROAT MAFIA I II
KING OF THE TRENCHES
By **Ghost**

LAY IT DOWN I & II
LAST OF A DYING BREED I II
BLOOD STAINS OF A SHOTTA I & II III
By **Jamaica**

LOYAL TO THE GAME I II III
LIFE OF SIN I, II III
By **TJ & Jelissa**

IF LOVING HIM IS WRONG…I & II
LOVE ME EVEN WHEN IT HURTS I II III
By **Jelissa**

PUSH IT TO THE LIMIT
By **Bre' Hayes**

IMMA DIE BOUT MINE 6 | ARYANNA

BLOODY COMMAS I & II
SKI MASK CARTEL I, II & III
KING OF NEW YORK I II, III IV V
RISE TO POWER I II III
COKE KINGS I II III IV V
BORN HEARTLESS I II III IV
KING OF THE TRAP I II
By **T.J. Edwards**

WHEN THE STREETS CLAP BACK I & II III
THE HEART OF A SAVAGE I II III IV
MONEY MAFIA I II
LOYAL TO THE SOIL I II III
By **Jibril Williams**

A DISTINGUISHED THUG STOLE MY HEART I II & III
LOVE SHOULDN'T HURT I II III IV
RENEGADE BOYS 1-4
PAID IN KARMA 1-3
SAVAGE STORMS 1-3
AN UNFORESEEN LOVE 1-3
BABY, I'M WINTERTIME COLD 1-3
A THUG'S STREET PRINCESS 1&2
By **Meesha**

A GANGSTER'S CODE 1-3
A GANGSTER'S SYN 1-3
THE SAVAGE LIFE 1-3
CHAINED TO THE STREETS 1-3
BLOOD ON THE MONEY 1-3
A GANGSTA'S PAIN 1-3
BEAUTIFUL LIES AND UGLY TRUTHS
CHURCH IN THESE STREETS
By **J-Blunt**

CUM FOR ME 1-8
An LDP Erotica Collaboration

BLOOD OF A BOSS 1-5
SHADOWS OF THE GAME
TRAP BASTARD
By **Askari**

THE STREETS BLEED MURDER 1-3
THE HEART OF A GANGSTA 1-3
By **Jerry Jackson**

WHEN A GOOD GIRL GOES BAD
By **Adrienne**

THE COST OF LOYALTY 1-3
By **Kweli**

BRIDE OF A HUSTLA 1-3
THE FETTI GIRLS 1-3
CORRUPTED BY A GANGSTA 1-4
BLINDED BY HIS LOVE
THE PRICE YOU PAY FOR LOVE 1-3
DOPE GIRL MAGIC 1-3
By **Destiny Skai**

A KINGPIN'S AMBITION
A KINGPIN'S AMBITION II
I MURDER FOR THE DOUGH
By **Ambitious**

TRUE SAVAGE 1-7
DOPE BOY MAGIC 1-3
MIDNIGHT CARTEL 1-3
CITY OF KINGZ 1&2
NIGHTMARE ON SILENT AVE
THE PLUG OF LIL MEXICO 1&2
CLASSIC CITY
By **Chris Green**

A GANGSTER'S REVENGE 1-4
THE BOSS MAN'S DAUGHTERS 1-5
A SAVAGE LOVE 1&2
BAE BELONGS TO ME 1&2
A HUSTLER'S DECEIT 1-3
WHAT BAD BITCHES DO 1-3
SOUL OF A MONSTER 1-3
KILL ZONE
A DOPE BOY'S QUEEN 1-3
TIL DEATH 1-3
IMMA DIE BOUT MINE 1-6
DYING FOR LIKES
By **Aryanna**

A DOPEBOY'S PRAYER
By **Eddie "Wolf" Lee**

THE KING CARTEL 1-3
By **Frank Gresham**

THESE NIGGAS AIN'T LOYAL 1-3
By **Nikki Tee**

GANGSTA SHYT 1-3
By **CATO**

THE ULTIMATE BETRAYAL
By **Phoenix**

BOSS'N UP 1-3
By **Royal Nicole**

I LOVE YOU TO DEATH
By **Destiny J**

I RIDE FOR MY HITTA
I STILL RIDE FOR MY HITTA
By **Misty Holt**

LOVE & CHASIN' PAPER
By **Qay Crockett**

TO DIE IN VAIN
SINS OF A HUSTLA
By **ASAD**

BROOKLYN HUSTLAZ
By **Boogsy Morina**

BROOKLYN ON LOCK 1 & 2
By **Sonovia**

GANGSTA CITY
By **Teddy Duke**

A DRUG KING AND HIS DIAMOND 1-3
A DOPEMAN'S RICHES
HER MAN, MINE'S TOO 1&2
CASH MONEY HO'S
THE WIFEY I USED TO BE 1&2
PRETTY GIRLS DO NASTY THINGS
By **Nicole Goosby**

LIPSTICK KILLAH 1-3
CRIME OF PASSION 1-3
FRIEND OR FOE 1-3
By **Mimi**

TRAPHOUSE KING 1-3
KINGPIN KILLAZ 1-3
STREET KINGS 1&2
PAID IN BLOOD 1&2
CARTEL KILLAZ 1-3
DOPE GODS 1&2
By **Hood Rich**

THE STREETS ARE CALLING
By **Duquie Wilson**

STEADY MOBBN' 1-3
THE STREETS STAINED MY SOUL 1-3
By **Marcellus Allen**

WHO SHOT YA 1-3
SON OF A DOPE FIEND 1-4
HEAVEN GOT A GHETTO 1&2
SKI MASK MONEY 1&2
By **Renta**

GORILLAZ IN THE BAY 1-4
TEARS OF A GANGSTA 1/&2
3X KRAZY 1&2
STRAIGHT BEAST MODE 1&2
By **DE'KARI**

TRIGGADALE 1-3
MURDA WAS THE CASE 1-3
By **Elijah R. Freeman**

SLAUGHTER GANG 1-3
RUTHLESS HEART 1-3
By **Willie Slaughter**

GOD BLESS THE TRAPPERS 1-3
THESE SCANDALOUS STREETS 1-3
FEAR MY GANGSTA 1-5
THESE STREETS DON'T LOVE NOBODY 1-2
BURY ME A G 1-5
A GANGSTA'S EMPIRE 1-4
THE DOPEMAN'S BODYGAURD 1&2
THE REALEST KILLAZ 1-3
THE LAST OF THE OGS 1-3
By **Tranay Adams**

MARRIED TO A BOSS 1-3
By **Destiny Skai & Chris Green**

KINGZ OF THE GAME 1-7
CRIME BOSS 1-4
By **Playa Ray**

FUK SHYT
By **Blakk Diamond**

DON'T F#CK WITH MY HEART 1&2
By **Linnea**

ADDICTED TO THE DRAMA 1-3
IN THE ARM OF HIS BOSS
By **Jamila**

LOYALTY AIN'T PROMISED 1&2
By **Keith Williams**

YAYO 1-4
A SHOOTER'S AMBITION 1&2
BRED IN THE GAME
By **S. Allen**

TRAP GOD 1-3
RICH $AVAGE 1-3
MONEY IN THE GRAVE 1-3
CARTEL MONEY 1&2
By **Martell Troublesome Bolden**

FOREVER GANGSTA 1&2
GLOCKS ON SATIN SHEETS 1&2
By **Adrian Dulan**

TOE TAGZ 1-4
LEVELS TO THIS SHYT 1&2
IT'S JUST ME AND YOU
By **Ah'Million**

IMMA DIE BOUT MINE 6 | ARYANNA

KINGPIN DREAMS 1-3
RAN OFF ON DA PLUG
By **Paper Boi Rari**

THE STREETS MADE ME 1-3
By **Larry D. Wright**

CONFESSIONS OF A GANGSTA 1-4
CONFESSIONS OF A JACKBOY 1-3
CONFESSIONS OF A HITMAN
CONFESSIONS OF A DOPE BOY
By **Nicholas Lock**

I'M NOTHING WITHOUT HIS LOVE
SINS OF A THUG
TO THE THUG I LOVED BEFORE
A GANGSTA SAVED XMAS
IN A HUSTLER I TRUST
By **Monet Dragun**

QUIET MONEY 1-3
THUG LIFE 1-3
EXTENDED CLIP 1&2
A GANGSTA'S PARADISE
By **Trai'Quan**

CAUGHT UP IN THE LIFE 1-3
THE STREETS NEVER LET GO 1-3
By **Robert Baptiste**

NEW TO THE GAME 1-3
MONEY, MURDER & MEMORIES 1-3
By **Malik D. Rice**

CREAM 2-3
THE STREETS WILL TALK
By **Yolanda Moore**

THE STREETS WILL NEVER CLOSE 1-3
By **K'ajji**

LIFE OF A SAVAGE 1-4
A GANGSTA'S QUR'AN 1-4
MURDA SEASON 1-3
GANGLAND CARTEL 1-3
CHI'RAQ GANGSTAS 1-4
KILLERS ON ELM STREET 1-3
JACK BOYZ N DA BRONX 1-3
A DOPEBOY'S DREAM 1-3
JACK BOYS VS DOPE BOYS 1-3
COKE GIRLZ
COKE BOYS
SOSA GANG 1&2
BRONX SAVAGES
BODYMORE KINGPINS
BLOOD OF A GOON
By **Romell Tukes**

CONCRETE KILLA 1-3
VICIOUS LOYALTY 1-3
BLOODY MONEY BAGS
By **Kingpen**

THE ULTIMATE SACRIFICE 1-6
KHADIFI
IF YOU CROSS ME ONCE 1-3
ANGEL 1-4
IN THE BLINK OF AN EYE
By **Anthony Fields**

THE LIFE OF A HOOD STAR
By **Ca$h & Rashia Wilson**

NIGHTMARES OF A HUSTLA 1-3
BLOOD AND GAMES 1&2
By **King Dream**

GHOST MOB
By **Stilloan Robinson**

HARD AND RUTHLESS 1&2
MOB TOWN 251
THE BILLIONAIRE BENTLEYS 1-3
REAL G'S MOVE IN SILENCE
By **Von Diesel**

MOB TIES 1-7
SOUL OF A HUSTLER, HEART OF A KILLER 1-3
GORILLAZ IN THE TRENCHES
OOPS CRY TOO 1&2
THE DAUGHTER OF A CARTEL BOSS
By **SayNoMore**

BODYMORE MURDERLAND 1-3
THE BIRTH OF A GANGSTER 1-4
By **Delmont Player**

FOR THE LOVE OF A BOSS 1&2
By **C. D. Blue**

KILLA KOUNTY 1-5
TENDER
By **Khufu**

MOBBED UP 1-4
THE BRICK MAN 1-5
THE COCAINE PRINCESS 1-10
STEPPERS 1-3
SUPER GREMLIN 1-4
A GANGSTA'S SON
By **King Rio**

MONEY GAME 1&2
By **Smoove Dolla**

IMMA DIE BOUT MINE 6 | ARYANNA

A GANGSTA'S KARMA 1-5
By **FLAME**

KING OF THE TRENCHES 1-3
By **GHOST & TRANAY ADAMS**

BAD BITCHES WIT GUNZ 1&2
PROBLEM SOLVED
By "Christopher Diesel" Hornezes

QUEEN OF THE ZOO 1&2
By **Black Migo**

GRIMEY WAYS 1-3
BETRAYAL OF A G
By **Ray Vinci**

XMAS WITH AN ATL SHOOTER
By **Ca$h & Destiny Skai**

KING KILLA 1&2
By **Vincent "Vitto" Holloway**

BETRAYAL OF A THUG 1&2
By **Fre$h**

COUNTDOWN OF A KILLA 1&2
SEX, MURDER AND GOD 1&2
GUNS DOWN, BOTTOMS UP 1&2
By Lo-Life

THE MURDER QUEENS 1-7
By **Michael Gallon**

FOR THE LOVE OF BLOOD 1-4
By **Jamel Mitchell**

IMMA DIE BOUT MINE 6 | ARYANNA

HOOD CONSIGLIERE 1&2
NO TIME FOR ERROR
By **Keese**

PROTÉGÉ OF A LEGEND 1,2&3
LOVE IN THE TRENCHES 1&2
By **Corey Robinson**

THE PLUG'S RUTHLESS DAUGHTER 1&2
By **Tony Daniels**

BORN IN THE GRAVE 1-3
CRIME PAYS
By **Self Made Tay**

MOAN IN MY MOUTH
By **XTASY**

TORN BETWEEN A GANGSTER AND A GENTLEMAN
By **J-BLUNT & Miss Kim**

LOYALTY IS EVERYTHING 1-3
CITY OF SMOKE 1-3
By **Molotti**

HERE TODAY GONE TOMORROW 1&2
By **Fly Rock**

WOMEN LIE MEN LIE 1-4
FIFTY SHADES OF SNOW 1-3
STACK BEFORE YOU SPLURGE
GIRLS FALL LIKE DOMINOES
NAÏVE TO THE STREETS
By **ROY MILLIGAN**

PILLOW PRINCESS
By **S. Hawkins**

IMMA DIE BOUT MINE 6 | ARYANNA

THE BUTTERFLY MAFIA 1-3
SALUTE MY SAVAGERY 1&2
By **Fumiya Payne**

THE LANE 1&2
By Ken-Ken Spence

THE PUSSY TRAP 1-5
By **Nene Capri**

DIRTY DNA
By **Blaque**

SANCTIFIED AND HORNY
by **XTASY**

BOOKS BY LDP'S CEO, CA$H

TRUST IN NO MAN
TRUST IN NO MAN 2
TRUST IN NO MAN 3
BONDED BY BLOOD
SHORTY GOT A THUG
THUGS CRY
THUGS CRY 2
THUGS CRY 3
TRUST NO BITCH
TRUST NO BITCH 2
TRUST NO BITCH 3
TIL MY CASKET DROPS
RESTRAINING ORDER
RESTRAINING ORDER 2
IN LOVE WITH A CONVICT
LIFE OF A HOOD STAR
XMAS WITH AN ATL SHOOTER